Independence  *rock*

Independence *rock*

DEBRA TERRY HULET

BONNEVILLE BOOKS
SPRINGVILLE, UTAH

This is a work of fiction. The characters, names, incidents, places, and dialogue are products of the author's imagination, and are not to be construed as real.

ISBN 13: 978-1-59955-441-9

Published by Bonneville Books, an imprint of Cedar Fort, Inc., 2373 W. 700 S., Springville, UT 84663
Distributed by Cedar Fort, Inc. www.cedarfort.com

LIBRARY OF CONGRESS CATALOGING-IN-PUBLICATION DATA

Hulet, Debra Terry, 1956-
  Independence Rock / Debra Terry Hulet.
      p. cm.
  Summary: In order to avoid juvenile detention, fifteen-year-old Katie
McBride, the daughter of an abusive alcoholic, goes on a "handcart trek"
that mimics that of the Mormon pioneers, and, in addition to finding and
reading the journal of one of her ancestors, she also finds friendship,
self-respect, and faith.
  ISBN 978-1-59955-441-9
  [1. Alcoholism--Fiction. 2. Child abuse--Fiction. 3. Mormons--Fiction. 4.
Frontier and pioneer life--Fiction. 5. Diaries--Fiction. 6. Utah--Fiction.]
  I. Title.

  PZ7.H885In 2010
  [Fic]--dc22

          2010019533

Cover design by Danie Romrell
Cover design © 2011 by Lyle Mortimer
Edited and typeset by Heidi Doxey

Printed in the United States of America

10 9 8 7 6 5 4 3 2 1

Printed on acid-free paper

To my children,
Carolina, Alejandra, Andrea, Landon, and Ciara,
who have become a great blessing to me as promised.
And to Him who gives all blessings.

Prologue

Back in the day—a generation ago—an announcement would come on at 10:00 p.m. every night on the local TV channel. Katie's father had told her about it. Sometimes interrupting a commercial or TV program, a male voice said the same thing to parents each night: "It's ten o'clock. Are your children at home?" Well, it was past ten o'clock. It was past midnight. And Katie's mother still hadn't come home.

Katie turned off the movie she was watching and looked out the sitting room window and down the blackened street. Most of the street lights were burned out. One just in front of her house, though, stretched a faint yellow glow over their splintered picket fence and patches of blown-out dandelions. Their yard always looked so ugly. *If I had a can of white paint,* thought Katie, *I just might paint the fence myself.* She laughed a little to think of how shocked her friends would be if they saw her painting. She wondered if any of them would offer to help. Maybe Gustavo would. But there was no money for a can of paint. No money for anything.

Now it was 12:15. Katie's mother had never come home this late before. Her mother wasn't a good driver—ever. Driving after staying out this late partying, though, was especially dangerous. Katie's mother always drove the car home, no matter how bombed she was. One night, as she pulled the car into the driveway, she ran into one of the poles that held up the carport.

It collapsed on top of the car. A huge dent, more like a crater, on the left side of the hood and scratches everywhere evidenced the end of the carport, but Katie's mother wasn't hurt.

"Stupid thing!" she yelled as she stepped out of the hand-me-down Ford. "I told your father this carport wouldn't last when he put it up. And now, look! I'm lucky to be alive!"

What if tonight her mother had accidently driven into a ravine or run a red light and smashed head-on into another car? Where would she go if something happened to her mother? She had no relatives she knew of. *Do they put fifteen-year-olds in orphanages?*

Katie watched now as headlights neared. It was the Ford. Running quickly into the living room, Katie pushed "play" on the remote, grabbed her potato chip bag, and sat on the floor in front of the couch. She didn't want her mother to know she was watching for her.

Katie heard the loud creak of the door and turned to see her mother steady herself on the entryway table. After stumbling twice as she made her way across the living room, Katie's mother leaned heavily on the back of the couch.

Then she noticed her daughter sitting on the floor. "Katie! What are you doing? You know you have school tomorrow! Can't I leave you alone for . . . for . . . even a minute?" She brushed her hair out of her eyes and dragged away a loose strand stuck to the bright red lipstick on her thin lips. "How dare you . . . how, how dare you . . . stay up this late!" She stopped talking, dropped her purse on the couch, and stared at Katie.

"I was . . . well, the truth is that I was waiting for you to get home. You . . . you really shouldn't drive when you've been drinking, Mom. What if you have an accident?"

"How dare you tell me wha—what I should do! I'm your . . . your mother!" she stammered, looming above Katie in tall, heeled boots.

Katie, sitting cross-legged on the floor, couldn't get away fast enough. She just didn't see it coming. A moment earlier her mother had appeared too weak and dizzy to harm a fly. Now she was a seething, potent black widow, and Katie, cornered by the couch at her back, was the fly in her mother's web. Kicking and slapping her over and over again, years of bottled anger smashing open, her mother ranted irrationally and spouted obscenities that Katie had never even heard before. Katie had never been so frightened in her life. While drunk, her mother had hit her more than a few times before, but this was different. This was a nightmare.

Katie searched her mother's face for the mom who used to sing to her at night as she lay in bed or the mother who years ago hugged her tight and smoothed her hair before Katie ran out to wait for the bus. That mom was gone. This mother's eyes spit hate, and her face stretched to strangle Katie.

She crawled around her mother's legs and scrambled along the splintered floor, her mother flailing kicks behind her. Katie was finally able to get up and run into her room. She slammed the door just as her mother fell into it and began pounding and yelling for her to open up. The phone lay on the bed where Katie had left it. With her weight against the door—there was no lock—she leaned over and snatched the phone. The kicks on her thighs ached, and her face bled. She called 911.

Before it began to ring, though, Katie quickly pushed the off button. *If I call the police,* she thought, *they'll take me away. They'll put Mom in jail. Dad's already gone. I won't have anyone left. And if Dad comes back, I won't be here.* A picture of her father smiled at her from atop the chest of drawers across the room.

Katie held her back to the door for the next five minutes until her mother stopped banging and slumped to the foot of the door. When she was sure her mother had either passed out or fallen asleep, she grabbed her pillow and the old, thick blanket at the foot of her bed and climbed out the window as she had many times before.

Stuffing the pillow and blanket into the lower branches of the backyard tree, Katie swung up. Her left thigh ached so much from the beating that she had to drop back down and try again. Once up in the tree, she pushed her pillow and blanket through the door of her tree house and climbed in. As she'd grown older and bigger, the tree house seemed to shrink. She couldn't even stretch out straight on the floor anymore. Still, Katie arranged her pillow and blanket on her habitual spot on the board floor, now slick with use. She sunk her head into the pillow and stared up into the night sky. From the spot where she lay, she could just see through the crack between two slats in the roof. It was not, however, a good place to lie in a rainstorm.

Dad said he was going to fix it, thought Katie. *That's not going to happen. He's not coming back—ever.* Tears slid out the corners of Katie's eyes and onto her pillow. She closed her eyes and saw herself reaching as high as her six-year-old self could, standing on the tips of her toes, to hand nails to her dad as he built the floor of the tree house.

"This will be our special house, Kate. And whenever you need me, I'll be here. You just tell me when, and I'll be here."

Sure, sure, Dad. Sure you'll be here. You never even call me.

This time Katie's tears fell onto the floor of the little house, and, after a long while, she slept.

One

Gazing at Katie over the top rim of his reading glasses, Judge Bellows appeared disgusted. In fact, he looked at her just as he would examine a foreign object, slimy and nasty-looking, that he had just found in his bowl of Wheaties. Fishing the object out, the judge spoke to it.

"What do you have to say for yourself, young lady?"

Katie felt like crawling under the Persian rug on the floor of the judge's office—like she was the lowest scum on earth. Seated in a wide, straight-backed, wooden chair directly opposite the judge's face, she looked down at her hands and twisted the tarnished ring on her finger slightly so that the small black stone lay centered. Katie's father had given it to her before he went away.

"Your grandmother gave me this ring," he had told her. "She said to give it to you when you were old enough to wear it. So hold on to it, baby, until it fits. Your grandmother said it has been in the family for generations."

I bet Dad never imagined the hand wearing this ring would slug Mom, thought Katie.

Her mother sat in a back corner of the judge's office under the American flag and a picture of George Washington kneeling by his horse. Her fair hair unusually pulled in a twist at the back of her neck, speaking only when spoken to, Mrs. McBride's answers were seldom more than "yes" or "no." She wore the only dress she owned, a white dress splattered with blue forget-me-nots. It was the same dress she wore on each of the two Sundays six years ago when she took Katie to church.

"Well, Katie?" asked the judge. "We're waiting." Indeed, Judge Bellows; Pam Collins, assigned as Katie's social worker; and a tall police officer, all looked at her expectantly. Even Katie's mother, who had heretofore kept her head lowered, looked up across the little room at her.

"My mother, well, she . . ." began Katie. She stopped, though. *They could still put my mom in jail,* thought Katie. *How long would they keep her in there? And where would I go? What would happen to me?*

"Yes? What about your mother?" he asked as he looked over at Mrs. McBride.

"Nothing," answered Katie weakly, averting her eyes from the judge's face. "Nothing. I really don't have anything to say."

Judge Bellows straightened himself in his chair. He appeared much taller now. "You are charged with causing bodily harm to your mother. I'm giving you a choice, Katie. Your first option is to spend time in a juvenile detention center—two months minimum. More, if your behavior there is not outstanding.

"As for your second choice, Miss Collins here may have had a bit of inspiration this morning. She knows I am always open to suggestions; I'm not the most conventional of judges," added Judge Bellows with a slow, deep chuckle. "Miss Collins's father is in charge of a unique, two-week pioneer trek being held to celebrate the 150th anniversary of the pioneer settling of our city. Before this hearing today, and with my approval, she contacted him. Mr. Collins has graciously consented to allow you—if you choose—a place with one of the handcarts, and it seems to me to be your best option. Miss Collins would make all the arrangements. The timing is perfect; school is out this Friday in your district, and the trek starts Saturday."

"Well, which will it be, Katie?" asked the judge sternly.

She looked straight into Judge Bellows's squinty eyes. "What's the trek going to be like?"

"It's a handcart trek, and, to be honest, it won't be easy. You'll be walking ten to fifteen miles every day, and you'll do your share of pulling the cart." The judge stopped to clear his throat and then continued. "It'll do you good, Katie. How about it?"

She thought for a few moments. "I guess I'll do the trek," Katie answered finally. "Will there be other kids my age?"

Judge Bellows smiled. He looked relieved. "Lots of kids your age. At least one hundred of them."

"Does the court have your approval, Mrs. McBride?" he asked.

And with the assenting nod of Mrs. McBride's head, the sentence became final.

That night Katie slept badly. Monstrous, hollow-eyed, and moaning creatures appeared, faded, and reappeared in dream after dream. They lurked under her desk at school, behind the shower curtain, and outside her window. The last monster Katie saw frightened her so much that she shot straight up in bed. From behind an old and weathered wooden door, a horrifying, misshapen duplicate of Katie herself lurched from the darkness. In what remained of the creature's decaying hand, it clutched an empty bottle of scotch.

Katie closed her eyes tightly and breathed deeply. *It's just a dream. It's just a dream. It's just a dream,* she repeated to herself. Sliding back down under her covers, she waited until her heart stopped jumping and then, noticing the daylight through her window, Katie held very still to listen.

She heard no sound from her mother's bedroom. That was good. If there was anyone she did not want to see this morning, it was her mother. Showering and dressing noiselessly and in record time—it took her just twelve minutes—Katie tiptoed out the door and headed toward the bus stop. She didn't bother to eat breakfast. She didn't know if she could find anything to eat in the kitchen, anyway.

At school, her head began to ache, and she wished that she would have at least looked around for a slice of bread or a glass of milk. To make matters worse, the annoying, one-minute warning song began sounding in the hallway as she walked to her second-period class. Students walking near Katie quickened their steps.

"Keep them dogies movin'—movin', movin', movin'!" blared the loudspeaker.

"Movin', movin', movin'. Yeah, I'm movin," Katie called to the speaker as she rolled her eyes high. "Do they think we're cows or something?" she complained loudly to a few students as they rushed by cautiously, gliding in a look-I'm-not-running attitude just in case a teacher or administrator appeared nearby.

Sure, this might cut down on tardies, thought Katie. *But we're not a stupid herd of animals. A song between classes would actually be kind of cool if the music they chose was halfway decent. Like some Red Hot Chile Peppers. Then the hallways would really rock. But Rawhide? It's just a scratchy theme song from an old western series.* Katie very much resented being treated like a farm animal.

As long as they're rounding us up, they might as well provide lassos and bullwhips for the teachers monitoring the hallways, thought Katie. She chuckled to herself as she imagined Mr. Black standing outside his classroom door cracking a bullwhip at the hustling behinds of passersby.

"Head 'em up, move 'em out, Rawhide!"

Katie slowed her pace as she recognized the end of the song. If she wasn't careful, she would move through her class doorway just as the tardy bell rang, and that was way too soon. *Slow down, Katie,* she warned herself. Why avoid making a scene?

There it was—the bell, finally. But the door was just a few yards away, and it was still too soon to walk in. Turning to a nearby locker, Katie began fiddling with the combination to buy time. Instantly the lock dropped open in her hand. *What have we here?* thought Katie. *See what happens when you hurry too fast to class? You forget to make sure your lock is shut tight, and someone like me gets into your locker! . . . someone like me . . . .*

Inside, just calling for her to take it, was a shiny blue iPod, complete with headphones. Katie examined the pictures plastered all over the locker. *I know whose locker this is! This is Laura Drummond's! Laura Drummond, the richest kid in the school.* Laura was in Katie's math class, and Katie knew for a fact that Laura's dad had just bought her a new generation iPod, smaller, light pink, and with twice as many gigs.

She won't even care, thought Katie. *And I can always put it back in her locker. She probably never shuts it tight.* Katie slipped the iPod into her backpack and headed toward the doorway to her class. *Everyone thinks I'm a criminal anyway. Especially after yesterday. I might as well act the part. Katie McBride, criminal at large.*

Sauntering into the classroom, she looked around. Mrs. Maxwell sat at her desk in the back. "Oops! Am I late again?" Katie sang out, dramatically opening her eyes and mouth wide in surprise and clapping her hand to her mouth.

"It would appear so, Katie," responded Mrs. Maxwell in a hushed voice as she continued marking the roll.

Several students paused their pencils and looked up at the commotion, but most recognized Katie's voice and simply continued writing in their journals.

Oh well, thought Katie, *you can't win every time.* Of course, she hadn't expected much of a reaction from Mrs. Maxwell. Actually, if any of her teachers could be called cool or even halfway normal, it would be Mrs. Maxwell.

Just in case anyone was still watching, Katie swung her head around as she walked toward her desk, a move that she knew called attention to her long black hair. Then, patting Brandon on the head and tapping Cammy's foot with her own as she made her way down the aisle, Katie finally sank into her chair and glanced up at the start-up assignment written on the whiteboard.

Journal Entry #45 (Last one of the year!)
If you could change anything in your life, what would it be? Explain your answer.

Katie slowly closed her eyes and ran her fingers through her hair. *What would I change? What would I not change would be a much easier question.* She laughed to herself.

The first thing I would do is erase yesterday, Katie thought. *To erase yesterday, though, I'd have to erase a lot more. I'd have to erase what happened a year ago—the night my mother kicked my legs black and blue with her boots. And then I'd have to erase all the times she smashed me after that. If I could just remember to get out of her way faster.*

Sighing deeply as she opened her classroom journal, Katie began writing. *Teachers never read these journal entries anyway,* she reasoned.

First of all, my dad would come back, and he'd never go away again. I'd change my mother, too, of course. She wouldn't drink anymore. And she would smile. Of course, she'd never hit me again. And then I wouldn't have to hit her either. I'd live in a nice house in a good neighborhood, and I'd do my homework every night.

Here Katie stopped her pen. It had never occurred to her before that she might want to do her homework. *I guess I would do it if I had a normal family,* she thought to herself.

Hmmm, what would I really be like if things were different? Katie wondered as she rested her chin in her hand. She was surprised then at how exhausted she suddenly felt. *I shouldn't be this tired. It's not even noon yet.* Katie felt soggy and colorless, like broccoli left boiling on the burner far too long. Folding her arms on top of the desk, she laid her head down and imagined herself in a different kind of life.

There I am right now. I step out of our SUV and wave good-bye, no, blow a kiss, to my mother. She blows a kiss back at me and drives away happily, her sunglasses (which I picked out for her) flashing very coolly in the morning sun.

My friends are all waiting for me on the grass outside the

school. (There are at least eight of them.) After big, smiley hellos and hugs, we head toward the school entrance. Sean Adamson is standing close by, and when he sees me with my heavy book bag, he is right there at my side and offers to carry it for me. He asks me if I'd like to hang out with him on the weekend. As we pass through the front doors, the sun rises high in the east, transforming the bricks of the school into bars of gold.

Now Katie laughed her laugh. The stupidity-of-it-all laugh. The this-is-it-Katie-darling-and-there-ain't-no-more laugh that was becoming more and more frequent for her. She let her eyelids slowly sink down to shut out her thinking and then squeezed them once tightly to stop any tears. Letting her eyes roll, she caused her mind to blank.

"Hey, Katie." It was Mrs. Maxwell. She opened her eyes to find the teacher kneeling by her desk.

"Hey," she replied, her voice void of any feeling.

"Bad morning?" the teacher softly questioned. Katie's only reply was to lower her eyelids and roll her gum over with her tongue to give it a slow chew.

"See me after class, okay?"

"Okay," Katie mumbled.

She tried hard for the next forty-five minutes to pull herself up again, but it was impossible. She just didn't seem to have the strength to reach down inside and lift out a laugh, a clever remark, or a sarcastic smile.

There was even a perfect opportunity. Small class groups were doing frozen depictions of images from the poem "Invisible." Brittany, Kim, and Carl held pointing arms and fingers motionless in the air as they stifled mute, mocking laughs with their free hands. The object of their pointing fingers, practically perfect Patricia Samuels, sat still, her knees pulled up almost to her chest, her face hidden as her head bent to her knees. She had her arms locked solidly around her ankles. It was actually quite impressive. But then it happened. Practically perfect Patricia fell over. The problem was that Patricia's pose happened to be from on top of a desk. So when she fell, she fell far and fast.

Everyone jumped up at once. A few even ran to Patricia's aid. However, there was no need for concern: Patricia looked up and smiled. She was fine.

Whoa, Patty, thought Katie, *what are you going to do next for laughs, huh?* or even *Hey, Pat, good thing you're fat—thick padding always helps ease a fall!* But as soon as each thought occurred to her, it slithered back down and died in her stomach. She simply didn't feel up to it today.

Katie certainly didn't feel like talking with anyone after class, either. Before the ending bell, she came up with a plan to slip out quickly, without Mrs. Maxwell noticing. But for some reason, a few seconds after the bell rang, Katie was still at her desk. She didn't know why. Maybe it was because she actually liked Mrs. Maxwell. Maybe it was because she didn't have the pick-up-and-go to get going. But there she was.

Positioning herself into the desk adjacent to Katie's, Mrs. Maxwell hesitated before speaking. "You weren't in class yesterday, Katie. I hope you weren't sick," she finally said.

"No, Mrs. Maxwell. I wasn't sick. I was in juvenile court." This didn't seem to be what Mrs. Maxwell expected to hear. She sat silent, concerned and still.

Silent conversations were always stressful to Katie, so she blurted out the truth. "What happened is that my mom hits me, and sometimes she beats me up. I think about calling the cops afterwards, but I never do. The night before last, she was really mad—and she was crazy drunk. She was going after me, so this time I hit her first. I beat her up before she could beat me up. She was the one who called the cops."

The teacher said nothing. She appeared not to know what to say.

"That's where I was," added Katie. "At juvie."

Mrs. Maxwell finally spoke. "Oh," was all she said. Then, "I'm sorry." But she looked like she meant it.

Katie straightened in her chair and tried to smile. She didn't want anyone feeling sorry for her. "It's okay. I don't have to go to jail or anything. I just have to go on some stupid two-week pioneer trek. The judge said it would"—and here Katie lowered her voice in a deep-throat parody of the judge's—"'do me good.'" With slender fingers, she signed extra large quote symbols too, just for effect.

"So," Katie said as she stood up, "can I go to my next class now? I'll be late."

"Sure. Go to class now," replied the teacher. And then in a softened tone, she added, "Let me know if I can do anything to help."

Katie didn't bother replying to that. As if a teacher would or even could do anything to help her with the mess her life had always been and always would be. "Bye, Mrs. Maxwell," she said simply.

"Wait, Katie," Mrs. Maxwell called as Katie walked to the doorway. "Don't you want me to write you a late excuse for your next class?"

"No . . . thanks, anyway," called back Katie, already out the door.

Arriving home that afternoon, she stopped to gaze at her reflection in the tarnished mirror that hung on the wall just inside the front door. The mirror reminded Katie of herself and of the chain of grandparents and great-grandparents who had ultimately given her life. Stained with dark smears, fissured around the corners and clouded over, the entryway mirror and Katie's family were very similar. In fact, the mirror and its destiny of deterioration probably began right here on this wall when Katie's ancestors, who built the home, placed it there. Had the mirror not been cared for as it should, or was it just that the natural state of all things, whether living or not, is eventual ruin? Katie thought "ruin" would describe her family perfectly.

"I'm home," she called out halfheartedly, never losing contact with the reflection of her own dark eyes in the mirror. Katie held still for a few seconds as she often did when she came home from school. She listened for footsteps—for maybe her dad's footsteps—or for the sound of his voice or her mother's calling back to her. Really, though, Katie expected no reply. And there was none.

Two

"Just look how this . . . this mountain man tries to carry on with Katherine!" exclaimed Marsha. "I'd as soon have an Indian be our wagon team captain."

"Not to interrupt, but I'm afraid we need to walk faster, Marsha," said Phoebe. "I believe we're falling behind." Marsha, a large woman, was already slightly out of breath.

They quickened their pace through the soft dirt until they came alongside Phoebe's wagon.

"Last night around the campfire . . . well, no, never mind," decided Phoebe. "'Whoso keepeth his tongue keepeth his soul from troubles,' you know." She pulled her lips tight and, with resolve, looked straight ahead as she continued walking. "That's Proverbs 21:3," she added.

"Phoebe Eliza James! When has that—" But here Marsha's voice became rough and she had to clear the wagon dust from her throat. With one last "hurrumph" she continued. "Phoebe, when have thoughts of 'whoso keepeth his tongue' stopped you before?"

Phoebe looked straight forward without responding. She pulled her handkerchief up over her nose and mouth.

"In your entire recollection, Phoebe, do you ever recall me witholdin' information from you, my closest and dearest friend? Did I or did I not let you know before it was announced that we were to all depart Nauvoo?"

"You did, Marsha."

"And when your husband was seen walking Mrs. Granger home, was I or was I not the first person to tell you?"

"All right, then." Lowering her handkerchief, Phoebe took a deep breath through her dust-clogged nose and let the air out in a loud sigh. "It just so happens that last night as some of us were seated around the campfire, Nathanial Atkinson ever so slyly put his arm around Katherine's shoulder. Marsha, you know me. I'm no busybody. I tried to divert my eyes, but I could not help but see what happened next."

"What did happen next, Phoebe? I would not be disappointed if she slapped him. Michael was the finest man I have ever known, and Katherine is devoted to his memory," huffed Marsha, trying hard to keep up with her friend's pace.

"She looked extremely uncomfortable. She sort of wiggled her shoulders and then said something to him. She obviously asked him to take his grimy arm off of her because that is just what he did."

"Perhaps he will finally get it into his simple head that she is not interested."

"But, wait, Marsha—there's more. Sam took up his fiddle, and dancing began. Katherine danced a polka with Brother Atkinson, and then, when they finished and were standing there all out of breath, he tried to kiss her. Marsha—with my own eyes I saw him lean over as if to kiss her on the cheek right there and then."

"And what did she do?"

"Well, what could she do? She turned and walked away."

Marsha stared at Nathanial Atkinson with as much disgust as she could muster. "Why, in heaven's name, they would choose a ruffian such as him with no sense of propriety to be our captain remains a total wonder to me."

"And to me, Marsha, dear. And to me."

"Look, Phoebe, Katherine has dropped her handkerchief," said Marsha, bending over with a little difficulty to pick it up.

"Katherine! Your handkerchief!" Marsha called out as she waved it in the air.

"Oh, thank you!" said Katherine, looking back. She handed the reins of her team of horses over to Nathanial and walked back toward Phoebe and Marsha. Taking the handkerchief, Katherine asked, "Have you seen my little boy? He was around the wagon just a minute ago!"

"No," said both ladies as they turned their heads to look for him.

"Perhaps he's with his friend's wagon?" suggested Phoebe.

"No, no, I don't think so," responded Katherine.

"Isaac!" she called loudly as she walked quickly back to Nathanial and her team. "Isaac! Where are you?"

"I'm right here!' he called to her as he ran close.

"Isaac! You know that I can't see you through all of this dirt the wagons are stirring up. You have to stay close by! I've told you that a hundred times!"

"A hundred, Mama?" Isaac asked. With Isaac, everything always had to be exact.

"Well, maybe not a hundred, but I know I've told you many, many times. Actually, maybe I *have* told you a hundred times! I'm sure I've told you at least two or three times each day since we left Winter Quarters."

"Maybe so," he replied.

"Look, Isaac. You can't even see the wagon in front of us! Just yesterday Sister Lewis and Sister Thompson went off looking for buffalo chips and were lost until this morning. So stay close to the wagon and stay close to me. Do you understand?"

"But sticking with you is so boring. There aren't any horned toads or beetles or anything on the trail. The oxen and the horses and the wheels smash them all."

"How 'bout a bird's eye view then, boy?" Nathanial offered, swinging Isaac up onto his shoulders. "Watch for movement, and if you see something, we'll run and nab it. All right?"

"All right!" replied Isaac excitedly. He began rotating his gaze just like a seaman might do as he looks for land from atop a captain's perch. This perch was high too. Nathanial stood more than six feet tall.

Katherine laughed. "If you spy any water, Isaac, be sure to shout it out immediately. You know, kind of like, 'Land, ho!' But instead you could say, 'Water, ho!'"

Isaac giggled. Katherine loved his giggle; it fell sort of like a waterfall and ended with a little upward catch. His laugh somehow reminded her of a small wiggling rainbow trout.

"I wonder when it's going to rain, Nathanial. This eternal dust is maddening," said Katherine. "Have you noticed my grandmother's trunk in the back of the wagon? The carvings are thick with dirt. I don't know if I'll ever be able to get it clean. The earth would pack down a little if it rained."

"You'll be changing one hardship for another though, Katherine. When it rains, these trails run thick with mud. I guarantee you'll like that even less."

"Hmmm. You could be right about that. The animals can hardly pull the wagons now, what with the heat and the dust; we only made eight miles yesterday. I imagine, though, that it may be even more difficult for them to pull through mud."

"Like flies strugglin' across warm butter, Katherine. And draggin' slabs of bacon behind 'em."

"Nathanial, you do make the strangest comparisons," chuckled Katherine. "I can just see the poor little flies now."

"If it makes you laugh, Kate, then it's a good comparison, whether it makes sense or not."

Kate. That's the second time he's called me Kate. Only Michael ever called me Kate before. If I were being true to Michael, I would tell him not to use that name. So why don't I?

They walked for a few minutes in silence. "See anything up there yet, Isaac?" asked Nathanial.

"Nope, not yet."

"Where's your bosom buddy Joseph today?"

"They took him up in their wagon. His mother said this morning before we broke camp that he couldn't walk with me today. He's sick."

"Has he got the fever?" Katherine asked, worried.

"Maybe. His mother said he had a fever during the night."

Katherine looked at Nathanial and then again at Isaac. "You and Joseph weren't drinking from mud holes, were you?" Katherine asked.

"No, Mother. You told me not to. Me and Joseph don't want to get sick. He'll get better soon, won't he?"

"'Course he will," answered Nathanial, and he began bouncing his stride to make Isaac laugh. "The two of you will be searching for lizards again before you know it."

Belying Nathanial's optimism were the shallow graves that too often lay at short distances from the trail. A procession of rock-lined graves floated through Katherine's mind. Graves without names. Graves that were often torn apart by hungry wolves or obscured by the winds and never again found. Katherine had heard the stories.

She would probably never have thought it possible to go west if Nathanial, a long-time friend of Michael's, hadn't promised her that he would make sure she and Isaac crossed safely. Since the trek was even more risky than Katherine had imagined at the outset, she felt very fortunate to have his help, though his interest in her was confusing. At times it seemed as if Zion were just an illusion—as if the wagon train had no real destination, no real end except to be slowly swallowed up by the wilderness. And to be responsible for Isaac as she followed a dream that was no more concrete than a warm feeling, seemed an immense task.

Will we ever get to Zion—alive? So many are dying along the way. And will it truly be worth it all?

They heard sharp cries up ahead, and the train of wagons slowly came to a stop. With hands on her hips and her pregnant belly ballooning, Sarah Brighton stood still alongside the wagon in front of them, her bonnet swinging softly behind her in the slow breeze. She seemed a faded gingham statue almost lost in stretches of dry earth and drier grass. Her husband, Sam, stood beside her, his scraped and ragged leather boots still amid the sagebrush. His hand faintly caressed the neck of his horse. Both Sam and Sarah looked ahead to the west to see what could be the cause of the standstill.

"Do you see anything, Nathanial?" Katherine asked. A huge, hazy, encircling column of dust was all there was to signify the wagon train ahead.

"No, I think I'll ride up and take a look."

"Sam!" he called out. "Take charge of the ten wagons for a while, will you?"

Nathanial untied his horse from the back of Katherine's wagon and rode off quickly.

A few people from the wagons nearest Katherine's gathered near hers. "Have Indians stopped us?" asked Phoebe, voicing everyone's fear.

"Isaac," said Katherine. "Go inside the wagon. I'll be there in a minute."

He began walking slowly, dragging a stick behind him.

"Go on, Isaac. Quickly!" ordered Katherine.

With Isaac up in the wagon now, Marsha spoke quietly. "We certainly have been blessed thus far," she said. "Hardly have we seen an Indian. I doubt, though, that the Lord will keep them away from us the whole length of the way." Some nodded their heads in vague agreement.

"This land has always been theirs," commented Sarah Brighton. "They can only see us as a threat."

"And we have miles and miles of their land to cross," added another.

"Nevertheless, we will trust in the Lord. We must," said Sarah.

After a minute or two of silence, Marsha spoke again. "I heard tell of a group of wagons bound for California." She stepped further from the wagon and continued in a hushed voice. "Indians stole into the camp during the night and took a child. A little two-year-old girl. They held a knife to the mother's throat."

The eyes of the women in the group grew wide, and the men's faces tightened as Marsha continued. "She screamed as the Indians left the wagon, and some men in the camp set off after them. They lost the Indians, though. Their horses were faster, and there was no moon. At daybreak, the men followed the Indians' tracks, but the hoof prints were lost in the river. The men couldn't find them again."

Katherine looked toward the wagon. "Marsha, you'll frighten Isaac!" she protested. "He might be able to hear you! Please, no more Indian tales. As far as we know, that's all they are—just tales."

Marsha shrugged her shoulders.

"Do you know for sure, Sister Marsha, that this really happened?" asked Sam Brighton. "Stories pass from one person to another on a wagon train, you see, and they often get worse in the tellin'."

"Brother Brighton," began Marsha, narrowing her eyes. "There were five wagons that quit the trail and returned to Missouri. They told the story to my sister Trudy. You can believe it or not. It's all the same to me." Offended, she walked off to her wagon.

Nathanial returned, his horse at a slow trot, and dismounted slowly. Isaac jumped quickly from the buckboard.

"What is it, Nathanial? Are Indians attacking?" Isaac asked.

"No, Isaac. It's . . . well, it's Joseph. Somehow he fell out of their wagon." In a quiet voice, he added, "He was hurt by one of the wheels."

"Will he be all right?" asked Katherine.

"They think he'll recover, but he's in quite a bit of pain. He's a strong boy, Kate, he'll mend quickly."

"He will. I'm sure he will," she responded. "Don't worry, Isaac."

Katherine lifted him up, and Isaac wrapped his arms tightly around her neck. "Everything will be all right. Joseph is in the hands of the Lord," she reassured him.

"But I don't see the Lord, Mama. I don't see his hands. Joseph is my very best friend. What if he dies?"

"Remember the quail, Isaac?" asked Katherine, recounting the incident as much for herself as for her son. "Aunt Rosemary and Uncle William were dying at Montrose, you know. They had nothing to eat and drink except corn and river water. It was very cold too, Isaac. Your aunt and uncle had only a thin little tent and one blanket to keep them warm. It seemed the Lord had forgotten them all. But he showed them he hadn't.

"One morning, completely out of nowhere, flocks of quail flew into the camp. And they didn't just fly around. It seemed they wanted to be eaten, for they dropped their plump little bodies right on top of and underneath the wagons. Why, some of them even dropped themselves right onto the breakfast tables! And they were so easy to catch just with bare hands. Those fat little quail made the first good dinner Aunt Rosemary and Uncle William had eaten in a very long time."

"And then after dinner, as if that had not been enough, the quail came back. Flocks and flocks of them! They would fly around the camp, very close, and then sit right down by the camp, just begging to be caught."

"Just like the quail that flew into the camp of the children of Israel after Moses led them out of Egypt! Right, Mother?"

"Yes, Isaac. Just like that. Both were miracles. The Lord remembered the children of Israel, he remembered our brothers and sisters at Montrose, and he remembers us. He will remember Joseph as well." *Please, Lord, make it so!*

Katherine heard something then. It was like a whisper, like the slightest bending of the grasses of the plain to a breath of wind. She lifted her chin, turned her head toward the eastern sun, and stood silent, waiting. It was as if someone had called her name. And yet she knew no one had.

"What is it mother?"

"Nothing, Isaac. I . . . I . . . just thought I heard something."

Closing her eyes, Katherine once more turned toward the sun and waited. Again she had the distinct impression of someone calling her name. The call was gentle, but expectant. *What is it, Lord?* Katherine asked silently. But there was no reply.

"Katherine, are you all right?" asked Nathanial.

"Yes . . . yes, of course," she replied.

As the wagon train began rolling, Katherine took hold of the reins. "Alfred, Josephine, get up now!" she called to the horses as she tugged sharply.

Once before, almost ten years ago, she had sensed her name being called by an unseen presence in much the same way. One of Katherine's chores on the farm in Vermont where she grew up was to milk the cows every morning. Her father always woke her.

"Katherine, my girl," he'd say, "time to rise and shine!'

She would crack her eyes open to see her father's morning smile. Katherine loved that smile. It was full of anticipation and carried with it a promise: that the day would be magnificent. She told herself that the man she married would have that same smile.

By the time Katherine made it out to the barn, her father would have already split open a bale of hay and would be spreading it out in the feeding troughs.

On one particular morning, she was reluctant to get out of bed and came dragging herself into the barn with her eyes half-closed. "You look tired, Katherine," her father said to her. "You didn't stay up drawing late last night, did you?"

Katherine yawned. Changing the subject, she asked, "How's Anabelle this morning, Pa? Is she still limping on her cut leg?"

"You did, then!" her father surmised with an attempt at a reprimand in his voice. Katherine's father never got angry at anyone. "How can I wake you before the sun's up if you're up all night drawing? Besides, I'll have to sell Anabelle and maybe Gracie and Tabatha too, just to pay for the oil you're burning up every night!"

"All right then, just for you, Papa," responded Katherine. "What if I draw for just an hour at night?"

"That will be much better. And, yes, Anabelle's leg is mending. She's standing strong on it this morning."

Katherine had said hello to Anabelle, affectionately rubbing the star above her nose, and had just pulled the white enamel bucket under the cow's belly when she thought she heard someone call her name, simply. Turning her eyes toward the barn door, she heard it once more, this time closer to her thoughts, more urgent. Immediately a picture flashed into her mind of her baby brother, Joshua, in his bassinet, blue, unable to breathe.

Katherine ran.

"Katherine? " her father called, having also noticed the worried look on her face. "Katherine!" He followed quickly behind her.

Rushing into her parents' bedroom, the door slamming against the log wall, Katherine hurried to the cradle and tore the tangled blanket off the newborn. "Ma! Help!" she screamed as she frantically began blowing into the baby's blue lips.

Almost flying from the feather bed in her white nightgown, Katherine's mother sat the baby up and began thumping his back with the palm of her hand. But nothing happened. Frantic, she blew into his mouth repeatedly while her husband supported the baby's head, tears running down his face. When baby Joshua still did not respond, Katherine's father picked him up and thumped his back with some force. Suddenly Joshua began to breathe, the blue of his tiny face fading to white and then to pink. And then he cried—loud enough, Katherine imagined, to awaken even the neighbors in the next farmhouse. She had never been so happy to hear her baby brother cry.

Katherine felt blessed—very blessed. The immensity of God's love for her and for her family amazed her. That night she made a promise to God that she would always keep. She called it a covenant. She promised Him that she would always believe in Him and would always do the things He asked of her.

Now, years later, having begun a trek to a new home in the West, Katherine felt the same call to her mind and heart. This time, however, no image had appeared to her, and she noticed no urgency. Well, Katherine decided as she walked, if it means something, and if it is important, I'll know it.

Three

As was her custom, Katie pulled her bedroom chair to the window to watch the colors of late afternoon turn to those of night. This was her favorite time of day. Soon the peaks and vertical cuts of the mountain warmed and radiated, the intense pink and honey tones spreading from the tips of the mountain to the roofs of the houses below. Suddenly, as happened almost every night, the homes lit ablaze as if having received an authoritative word or catalyst, the windows magnifying and burning with the fire of the setting sun. Each home appeared apt to explode from within. And at the very base of the mountain, somehow oblivious to this wild conflagration, a line of headlights moved ever so slowly north and away along the old highway. Katie wondered why the drivers of those vehicles were not panicked by the fiery windows as they passed them by. Perhaps only she herself could see the blaze. Maybe it was a magic that was just for her. Or maybe not. How could there be a magic that was just for her?

"What's there? What are you looking at?" It was Katie's mother. She was drunk, as usual. Swaying slightly, she clung to the splintered door frame and to the tarnished brass handle of the door as she spoke.

"Nothing," answered Katie, her anger against her mother— but mostly against her mother's drunkenness—very apparent in her voice.

"I don't know why you have to be mad at me, Katie," complained her mother, resting her weakened body on Katie's bed. "I've tried so hard to be a good mother to you," she added with a telltale catch in her voice.

Oh, no, thought Katie. *Here it comes.* When her mother was drunk, she inevitably became one of two extremes: an angry monster—like she had become last year—or a sad, sobbing mess.

There was a time, several years ago, when her mother's drunken tears would move Katie to compassion. Apologizing to her mother repeatedly and pulling strands of pale hair away from her mother's eyes and mouth, Katie had done her best to help. She'd also struggled with a heavy burden of mistaken guilt; she had felt then that her mother's sickness was all her fault. Perhaps she was not a good daughter. Perhaps she didn't help her mother enough or maybe she complained too much. Perhaps she wasn't obedient enough or good enough somehow. Or maybe it was just the mere fact of being alive that caused her mother such pain.

But Katie tried not to think that way anymore. Her mother, while drunk, had slapped her, slugged her, and kicked her a few too many times now for such thoughts to remain. Now Katie figured it was time to look out for herself. If her mother chose to drink, then her mother would just have to live with her self-made misery.

Katie's mother, sprawled out over the bed, cried heavily now, her tangled blonde hair blending into the crocheted bed throw, the old cover that had once been on her parents' bed. Not long after Katie's father left, her mother gave it to Katie.

"This is your dad's old hand-me-down, probably handed down more times than I can count. Maybe you can fix it up." Loose crochet threads hung throughout the blanket near stretches of crochet holes. Discolored in many spots as well, the blanket needed a miracle; Katie's efforts would have little effect.

"Well, it's yours now. You can just throw it away as far as I'm concerned," added Katie's mother that day.

Now, years later, lying on that still-unrepaired bed throw, Mrs. McBride cried. "I don't know what more I can do. He didn't care! Your father didn't care one bit! He just took off and left me! Left me . . . and left you . . . and I've tried . . . I've . . . really . . . tried. . . ."

"Mom?" Katie said as she shook her mother's shoulder just to see for sure. Yes. As happened frequently, the scotch had knocked her out. Katie hoped she would awaken and move to her own bed sometime tonight, otherwise Katie would have to sleep on the couch. And since the couch was old, its springs were pokey and the whole thing was full of dust, so if Katie moved around too much, dust would fly up and make her eyes swell and itch.

Well, tomorrow was her sixteenth birthday, and she wasn't going to sit around babysitting her passed-out mother. Pulling on her party jeans and high-heeled sandals, Katie pulled hard on the front door—it often jammed—and pushed out through the screen, letting it creak shut behind her. She knew there was no way the creaking noise would ever register on her mother: she was just too far out of it. Katie smiled as she heard Ricky Martin blaring from a house down the street. *That would be Gustavo's house,* she thought. *What would Friday night be without Gustavo?* And she loved to dance, especially to Gustavo's Latin music.

"Hey, baby!" called out a friend as Katie walked up Gustavo's driveway.

"Hey. What are you doing out here? Is little Stevie scared to dance with the ladies?"

"Look who's talkin', Miss I-gotta-get-home-now," he replied. "I found your glass slipper, though, the last time you ran away before midnight; it's on the mantel inside the house."

"Well, I just better go get it then before you get to thinking it's yours and wear it to school!"

Stephen ran his long fingers through his bushy hair and tapped his cigarette. Smoldering ashes floated through the dark onto the cool, moist grass. "I would, you know," he finally said. "But I don't think I'll be at school tomorrow."

"That's right. I forgot. Your little ga-ang needs you," Katie replied in a saucy voice, stretching the word "gang" into two swinging syllables.

"You should come hang out with us sometime," said Stephen, ignoring her tone. "I kinda miss the good old days. Too bad you had to become too good for me. How about meeting up with us tomorrow night?"

Katie knocked on Gustavo's door. "Sorry, I can't," she said to Stephen as she stepped in. And then as he watched her enter the house, the light of his cigarette moving to his lips, she called back through the open doorway, "I don't have a gun!"

Some might be afraid to taunt a member of the Red Snake gang, but Katie wasn't. She had known almost every single one of them since they were little boys playing kick-the-can with her in their neighborhood. She had kissed Stephen on the cheek once on a dare when she was in fourth grade, and she had almost carried his friend Sam home once after he fell and cut up his knee on broken glass. How could you be afraid of your childhood friends?

As Katie looked around Gustavo's living room, though, her old friends did become rather frightening. Sam lay sprawled out across the floor, a huge smile spread across his face, his shirt open to the waist. He scratched incessantly at his face, his stomach, his arms—but he never stopped smiling. As though in a trance, her eyes immense bloodshot orbs, Katie's friend Melissa stared starkly at the light directly above her head. She whispered sporadically to someone or something that neither Katie—nor anyone else—could see.

Katie recognized a girl she had seen often in the hallways at school, a girl who always dressed as if she and a one-hun-dred-dollar bill had just spent the previous afternoon at the downtown mall. Whether in the hallways or in the cafeteria, she was almost always surrounded by so many other kids that you could only get a glimpse of her new sandals or a jewel in her ratted hair. Tonight she sat on the edge of the couch, her only companion a young man with a mustache who was tying a plastic band just above her elbow. She seemed nervous. With her shirtsleeve rolled up, the girl rested her arm on an end table under a dim lamp. The bare arm was bright-white and unblemished.

The house was crowded with bodies, some smiling and scratching like Sam, others laughing, talking non-stop, or shooting up like the one-hundred-dollar girl. It seemed almost as if Katie had been transported into some sort of crazed, surreal laboratory. A long-faced woman with huge dark rings under her eyes, probably in her forties, burned a lighter flame under the bowl of a silver spoon, while a young man across from her heated the bowl of a light bulb with his lighter and sucked at the smoke emanating from its open end. Flickering little lighter flames dotted the room, momentarily on and then off again, bouncing light off the needle points of syringes. The faces of those holding the flames lit eerily, contrasting starkly with the faces of those who received only the scanty light of a lamp half-drowned at the far side of the room. One tangled couple in the corner acted as if Gustavo's living area were a private bedroom: they seemed totally oblivious to their surroundings. Through the air that hung half-dead with a medicinal, smoky stench that at first made Katie feel nauseated, Ricky Martin repetitively and deafeningly blared out, "Living la Vida Loca." No one danced.

"Hey, baby! Come sit down by Gustavito," said Gustavo, patting the vacant seat next to him on the couch. His smile was welcoming, but he didn't look quite all there.

Of all her guy friends, Gustavo was the best-looking. Katie had always thought so. Tonight, though, his smile was a little crooked, his brilliant blue eyes dull and half-shut, his wavy hair a mass of dark disarray, and it didn't look like he could sit straight if he tried. Katie said "hi" and moved closer to him, but she did not sit down.

"We've got some good stuff tonight, girl! Sit right on down here, and we'll get you slammin'."

"I . . . I dunno, Gustavo."

"Baby, this little silver spoon will lead you to places of ecstasy you never knew existed. Trust me on this. "

Katie sat on the couch by Gustavo and thought back to the seventh grade. At lunch, she, her two best friends, and several other girls sat in a circle on the grass of the school grounds far away from the building. Someone lit a marijuana joint and began passing it around the circle. As Katie watched both her best friends inhale and smile, she thought of her mother's smile as her mom sipped her cheap scotch. And she thought of the violent person her mother often became a few drinks later. Katie was the only one in the group who did not smoke.

Having always been determined not to end up like her mother, Katie knew she would never drink. But as the years passed, she came to realize that failure was inevitable. No matter how hard she tried, or where she turned, she never had—nor ever would—do well. It was in her genes. It was in the black eyes and straight black hair she inherited from her father, the epitome of crash-and-burn, disappointment, and weaseldom. It was in the lines of her cheeks and the lift of her nose that came from her mother—her mother, who could never face reality, who swallowed herself up in alcohol to hide from life and from her own self. It was in the house Katie lived in, a dilapidated relic from generations of Katie's ancestors, ancestors who Katie guessed lived miserable existences full of bad luck and bad choices. That was Katie's legacy, and she had given up fighting against it. Besides, this was different than drinking.

Sinking deeper into the space by Gustavo, Katie smoothed her hair back, took Gustavo's arm, and asked quietly, "So, how do I get started?"

Before he could answer, however, the front and back doors blasted open with sudden force, and uniformed men covered with special gear streamed through the entry and the back entrance to the kitchen. It was something out of a movie.

"Get on the floor!" one of them shouted. "Spread your arms and legs out flat!"

"Down! Get down!" one large cop near her yelled as he shoved Gustavo hard to the floor.

Katie, almost unable to breathe, but knowing she must move, scrambled to the carpet. She crawled to an empty part of the floor and spread herself flat, skin-tight jeans, high heels, and all.

"You're all under arrest!" called out the first officer. "Put your mouths to the floor and your hands behind your backs! Now!"

Four

A perfectly round, storybook sun slid across the sky toward the spire of the Nauvoo temple. Spilling a magic translucency on the green of the guarding trees, over the moving fields of grass, and upon the dollhouse-like homes gathered below, the sun centered itself behind the solid white of the temple and, approving, sanctified it.

Katherine smiled in her sleep. She awoke to remember the pleasant scene she beheld in her dream and then slept again. This time, however, she dreamt of Michael.

He and Nathanial worked side by side in the limestone quarry, cutting stones for the temple. Michael placed his chisel in the hollow of a large seam of limestone and swung his hammer to meet it. The stone refused to split. Soggy heat sinking into the quarry, Michael stopped to wipe his forehead with a handkerchief. He arched his back to relieve the stiffness caused by constant bending and hammering.

Though Katherine was in their newly built, red brick home a mile away, he turned his black, Irish eyes to her and smiled. Katherine watched him and smiled back. She could not love him more. The temple would soon be complete and glorious, and she knew Michael was proud to be a part of its construction.

Then time slowed. Michael's movements became stilted, ponderous, and exaggerated, as did Nathanial's and those of the men working near them on the hillside—it was as if the inner movements of time had rusted. The calls of the men working in the quarry fell to a lengthened, deep droll as if they spoke from the depths of a chasm.

Katherine knew it was going to happen before it did. In her dream, she yelled to warn Michael, but the force of her scream propelled her backward into the feather mattress, and the warning was stifled. Katherine shifted her vision from her husband to James Tuttle, who stood on the hillside several feet above and to the left of Michael. As James's hammer lowered inch by inch to meet his chisel, Katherine panicked. She tried with all her strength to call out to James to stop the hammer. But no noise would leave her lips. She could do nothing.

The hammer met the chisel, and, just as Katherine knew would happen, a small piece of rock flew into the air. It flew toward Michael. In her dream, Katherine blew fiercely toward the flying chip to alter its course, but no air left her. And then it hit him. The rock struck with sudden violence at Michael's temple. Time quickened.

Katherine found herself suddenly by his side. Nathanial held Michael's shoulders and head up in his arms. But Michael was dead. Placing her hand at his temple to cover the bleeding wound, Katherine screamed once more.

Then she awoke. It was the same nightmare Katherine always had. But no nightmare, nor anything, would bring Michael back.

"Did you dream about Papa again, Mama?" Isaac asked as he lay by her side in the wagon. His mother's muffled crying in the night seemed to no longer frighten him.

"Yes, Isaac. I'm okay now."

"When will we see Papa again?"

Before responding, Katherine drew her son close to her and waited a moment to calm and slow her breathing.

"Soon, Isaac, soon," she finally said. "On the other side. Papa is just preparing the way for us. I can just imagine him building a huge castle for us to live in, can't you?"

"But why, Mama? Why did the Lord let the rock hit Papa's head? Why did the Lord let Father die?"

"I don't know, Isaac. . . . The Lord hasn't yet given me an answer to that question." Then, after taking a deep, long breath and letting it out slowly to gather her courage—and her faith—Katherine added, "But I do know God loves us and watches over us. And that is enough to know."

Apparently satisfied with his mother's reply, Isaac fell back asleep almost immediately. Katherine, however, lay awake, unable to sleep, until a soft glow of light appeared through the drawn curtains of the wagon.

Wishing to see the rising sun, she sat up in her makeshift bed, and, arranging her mother's shawl around her shoulders, she pulled the curtain aside and climbed out the back of the wagon.

Katherine loved the morning. She always had. Even those mornings when she had to get up before daybreak to milk the cows. And she especially loved mornings here on the plains. The cracked earth, cooled by the night and gently lit with the dawn, calmed Katherine's disquiet. From hidden clumps and distant trees, birds, rarely seen in the heat of the day, sang out in random compositions marked by brief but striking solo performances. Katherine, though she tried, could rarely identify the soloists. Sparrows and finches sporadically flew up from their places of rest to alight on other branches or bushes.

On mornings such as these, it was difficult for Katherine to find resentment toward the God who had taken her Michael home to Him. For on mornings such as these, the world was perfect, her heart brimmed full, and somehow even Michael's death fit into this sunlit, perfect world. She was not quite sure if this great exodus of latter-day travelers were really a migration of modern-day Israel, as some had said. Neither was she sure as others seemed to be that the unbelievers left behind would be destroyed as were Sodom and Gomorrah. But she did know one thing: Katherine believed without doubt in the Lord and in His love for her. There was no way she could not know it. It was part of her heart, impossible to extricate.

"'Tis the early bird catches the worm, miss, to be sure," spoke a quiet, hidden voice.

Swinging around, Katherine saw movement under the wagon. "Who's there?" she whispered.

"No one, really," answered the voice. "Only meself." With that, the owner of the voice awkwardly scrambled out from under the wagon, her frayed and split button-up boots first. She carried a very large prize out with her—a three-layer, foot-wide circle of buffalo dung.

"For certain, 'tis the early bird catches the worm, or would we say . . . catches the buffalo droppin's in this case?" The round little woman began laughing outright and then, realizing that she might wake those still sleeping, she quickly clapped her hand to her mouth, clutching the huge buffalo chip to her bosom with her free arm. The woman had forgotten, however, that the chip was not quite dry. She immediately wiped her mouth with the back of her hand and spat forcefully into the dirt. But then there was the problem of her apron. Pulling the chip slowly and hesitantly away from her chest, she saw that her fears were met. Her apron—what may have been her only apron—old and patched, was caked with dung.

Katherine knew she shouldn't laugh. But the old woman's round face, with her lips pursed and her eyes and forehead crunched to the center of her nose in dismay and disgust, was just too funny. Before Katherine could apologize for laughing, though, the old woman herself laughed out loud, bending forward and backward while she held her hand to her ample stomach. She laughed so loud that Katherine could not make her apology heard.

"Hey, what's going on?" asked Isaac, sticking his head out the wagon. "What's so funny?"

"Nothing really, Isaac. Nothing at all," answered Katherine, barely able to hold back further laughter. "Our friend here, though, has come upon a buffalo chip bigger than any I've ever seen! Just have a look, Isaac!"

"I see, Mama. And she truly has come upon it. It's come

upon her face and landed all over her apron!" giggled Isaac.

"Just so," agreed the old woman. "And you're a clever wee article, then, sure you are. I'll be needin' a pot of water to clean up this apron and wash me face. A large pot of water! Off wi' you now, no strollopin'! And be quick about it then!" she ordered, seeming to expect compliance.

Isaac, turning a questioning face to his mother and receiving a nod of her head in reply, pulled on his pants and scrambled quickly out of the wagon. He grabbed the water pot that hung at the buckboard and ran off toward the stream, the tail of his nightshirt fluttering behind him.

"You've raised a fine lad, sister," said the woman to Katherine. "The spittin' image of his father."

"His father?" asked Katherine in disbelief. "You knew his father?"

"Well, Katherine McBride is who you are, is it not? 'That over there is the wagon of Sister Katherine,' so the man said to me."

"Yes, yes, I'm Katherine. But you say you knew Michael?"

"Did I know Michael, says she," mumbled the strange woman, shaking her head at the silliness of the question. "Of course I knew Michael! Changed his diapers, I did!"

"Changed his diapers?" asked Katherine again in disbelief. "Just who are you?"

"Name's Madeline," answered the woman, thrusting her least dirty hand out to shake Katherine's. "Nursemaid, cousin, and all-around mother to your Michael."

"Maddie?" questioned Katherine excitedly. "Madeline McFarland?"

"The one and the same! Here I stand, ready to do your biddin'. And I do say it be more tryin' to find ye both than it be to cross an entire ocean! Aye, traveled to all arts and parts to find ye, I did. You weren't after thinkin' you could raise this boy on your own, were you now?"

"But how did you get here, Maddie? And how on earth did you know where we were?"

"'Tis a huge, sprawlin' country, indeed. Like our wee Ireland, sure 'tis not. I went in search of Nauvoo, though, knowin' that our God would lead me to you now. There they enlightened me as to your whereabouts. Some who had shared the cold with the both of ye at your Winter Quarters—I'm believin' the name of the family was Beal—knew also that ye had set off from there in the Hutching Company."

"Surely, though, you didn't come all this way along the trail by yourself?" questioned Katherine.

Maddie chuckled, a deep chuckle that shook her shoulders and belly. "Though I pride meself on me resiliency, Katherine," she responded, "such an undertakin' I could n'er attempt alone. I'm not a fool who's after findin' herself lost in this wilderness and dyin' for want of sustenance."

Sitting down heavily on a tree stump, Maddie continued. "But to answer your question, I'll be tellin' you that a man named Jackman took me with him to catch up to your company. Oh, what a fine man he is! Knows all about your Indians, where they're camped and how they think. I' faith the man can tell ye how to survive on weeds and dirt, he can. Six of us there were that traveled wi' him. A fine gentleman."

"I will find him and thank him," responded Katherine. "Oh, Maddie, you don't know what a blessing your coming is to me." Her eyes filling with tears, Katherine added, "Your memories of Michael will add to mine, and all the more I'll feel him with me."

So eager was Katherine to embrace Maddie—this new-found part of Michael's life—that she forgot completely about the smashed buffalo chip. Two aprons were washed in the wash pot.

"Michael spoke often of you, you know. Whenever he met anyone who had recently arrived from Europe, he would ask if you had been on the ship," commented Katherine as Maddie rubbed the soapy aprons back and forth together.

"And he always sang me a song at night to help me go to sleep," added Isaac. "He told me, 'Maddie sang this song to me.'"

"And e'er what song would that be, me laddie?" asked Madeline softly.

"I don't know the name of it. But there's a part of it that likes to run through my head. It sounds like this:

"'The green grass shall not grow
"'Nor the sun shed his light
"'Nor the fair moon and stars gem
"'The forehead of night.'"

"Ah—that would be 'The Young Man's Dream.' And me mam sang it to me, and I suppose her mam sang it to her. *'The stream shall flow upward, the fish quit the sea,'*" continued Madeline in a slightly croaky—but somehow beautiful—tone of voice. "Ere I shall prove faithless, dear angel to thee." Here she stopped, and they all met the end of her song with silence.

In the distance, however, the song seemed to be taken up again. Two or perhaps three voices at first, the chorus grew rapidly until it reached Katherine's wagon, filled the billowing top of Sam and Sarah Brighton's wagon, rolled through all the wagons of Katherine's group, and then echoed on through the camps behind them. It was not, though, "The Young Man's Dream."

The words became clearer with each added voice:

We'll find the place which God for us prepared,
Far away in the West,
Where none shall come to hurt or make afraid;
There the Saints will be blessed.
We'll make the air with music ring,
Shout praises to our God and King;
Above the rest these words we'll tell
All is well! All is well!

"You know, Madeline," said Katherine, "it is hard not to feel all is well with such a chorus rumbling over the countryside. It seems to echo right through me and take out every worry."

"Rumble it does," commented Madeline. "But how this company might remain content at all after the many tragedies which befall it, I'll never know. Ye Mormons are not like another; ye be a strange lot. I've said it before, and I'll say't again now."

"Strange, yes, Maddie. But with a great purpose."

"Have ye now?" asked Maddie. She rubbed her fists tightly together to get out a particularly deep stain. "'A great and glorious purpose,' says she. That well may be. I' faith, that entirely well may be. I do notice betimes the certain strength and peace which altogether differs with the rest of the lot of us."

"Maddie," began Katherine thoughtfully. "Why did you really cross the ocean and plains to find us? It wasn't truly because you thought I couldn't take care of Isaac by myself, was it? Why did you leave your beautiful Ireland?"

Maddie stilled her scrubbing fists for a moment, cleared her throat, and lifted her chin. "Michael's mam was the most lovely lass ye would e'er see in your life, she was. And her heart, now, was pure. Aye, she'd sooner give ye her last morsel o' bread and starve rather than see ye go hungry. Her only cousin, I was. When she grew sickly and passed to t'other side, her husband John suffered not like another. Lost his wits, he did. Couldn't so much as look at his wee little son without the tears runnin' down his cheeks. He asked meself if I wouldn't care for the boy. John left entirely then. Some said he went to Scotland. Some were after sayin' he died. The fact o' the matter is I never saw the man again, so it is."

"Michael said he loved you as he would his own mother," commented Katherine.

"I believe 'twas so, Katie. May I be callin' you Katie, then?"

Katherine smiled. "Of course you may."

"Well, then, Katie, I believe 'twas so," said Maddie. She rinsed the aprons in clean water she had saved in another bucket. "And sure, I cared for me Michael as I ever would o' me own son, now.

He grew, o' course, as boys will do, and traveled to the new country. Sure and I told me Michael I'd be comin' soon. Me mam, you know, was all alone she was, and needed someone to look out for her. The years passed and me mam passed on, God bless her soul, and determined I was to find passage on the next ship to America. No children I had of me own, you see.

"'Twas then," continued Maddie as she slopped the aprons through the rinse water one last time, "'Twas then and I happened upon a Mormon missionary and was told all about Michael's accident and you makin' your way west. I had no one at all left in Ireland, 'tis sure. So, and though me Michael was now with me mother, I decided a little adventure and a new life still held promise. O' course, me first desire here was to find ye and to know ye as ye are me only family in all the world." Isaac smiled as Maddie tapped him on the tip of his nose and tousled his hair.

"And we couldn't be more happy that you came, Maddie," responded Katherine.

Rolling up her sleeves, Maddie then wrung out the two aprons tightly and hung them over the buckboard to dry. Katherine had never seen a woman wring out clothing as tightly nor with such ease.

"Look now, though," said Maddie as she noticed a change in movement in the camp. "Some is hookin' up their livestock ahead. Hadn't you best be doin' the same?"

"Yes, Maddie. It appears it's time to move out. Are you able to drive a wagon?" asked Katherine.

"'Am I able to drive a wagon?' she asks. And me, the champion buggy racer of Londonderry, 'tis sure."

"Well, then, we can spell each other driving or leading the horses. Your companionship and assistance on our journey would be of great help."

"'Twill be an honor, m'lady, it will."

"But what about our breakfast, Mother? We've not had time to have breakfast," complained Isaac.

"Not to worry," rejoined Katherine. "I have corncakes made

just yesterday morning and dried apples to fill our stomachs, although I don't believe your stomach can ever be completely filled."

Isaac turned his head to the side, the ends of his copper-colored hair gleaming red now in the morning light, and tapped his fingers over his lips as he pretended to think on it. "No," he finally decided. "Don't think I've ever been full in six years. And that's my whole life!"

A few of the horses, pasturing in a lower, grassy area nearby, swung their heads up at the usual clanks and rustles that signified the break-up of camp. Katherine's lead horse, apparently in anticipation of once again hauling the wagon, dropped heavily to the ground and neighed loudly.

"That'll be Josephine," Nathanial called out as he neared the wagon. "Mornin' Katherine. Isaac. Mornin' ma'am," he said to Madeline, taking off his hat.

Katherine couldn't help noticing the way his hair shone golden in the sunlight. It looked like he just washed it in the stream. "Madeline," she said, discarding her thought, "this is Nathanial Atkinson, our team captain. Nathanial, Madeline McFarland was like Michael's mother and has come all the way from Ireland hoping to join us here," said Katherine.

Nathanial extended his hand to Madeline. "Happy to meet you, ma'am," he responded. "I'm sorry for your loss."

"I do be thankin' you, sir. But sure, and what can you do now?" she responded, shaking her head.

"Are you with one of the other teams, Mrs. McFarland?" asked Nathanial.

"I'm after arrivin' this mornin', I am. Made me journey with Mr. Jackman all the way from Missouri."

"Madeline will be traveling with us, Nathanial," explained Katherine. "Do you have bedding, Madeline?"

"So I have, to be sure, me girl."

Up in the distance, several wagons began rolling, and Josephine again neighed and snorted from her reclining position.

"Josephine hates the thought of pulling the wagon,"

Katherine explained to Madeline. "Sometimes I wonder if it isn't more difficult to get her harnessed than it would be to pull the wagon myself!"

"Let me help you," offered Nathanial. "I think Josephine kinda likes me."

She and Nathanial headed off in the direction of the horses, Katherine lifting her foot high before each step so that her boots would soak less morning dew. She picked up a heavy stick. "This just might come in handy," she said.

Before they reached Josephine, however, Nathanial saw something off to the right about forty yards that caught his attention. It was the skull of a large animal. The interesting thing was how it was set on the ground—not strewn flat, as bones will naturally be found—but propped up vertically against the land and against the baby blue of the morning sky.

"Look, Katherine!" he exclaimed. "Come this way! Do you see it? It looks like a marker; some of the earlier wagon trains left them along the trail."

As Katherine came closer, she saw that indeed, the skull was scratched with letters. Already somewhat faded by wind and rain, however, the lines were difficult to decipher. The wording looked like tracks of wandering worms.

"My guess, Katherine, is that this marker was left by Brigham Young's company."

Katherine squatted down by Nathanial in front of the skull. Tracing her fingers along the top line, she tried to make out the writing. "I believe it says 'From North Platte River' and then '32' or maybe '52 miles.' The number is really impossible to read."

Then, as she traced her fingers again and again over the lower wording, trying to make out a name, something happened. It was at first small—a sharp piercing warmth inside of her—but it soon began to spread and branch until it warmed and filled her and there was no more space to fill.

Nathanial began talking—something about a wagon train . . . William Clayton . . . what? Nothing made sense.

What she felt brought to her mind the strange whisper of her name that she had felt more than heard several days earlier. It seemed a connection, a pull, a tie. But to what? To the past? To those who had written the lines she was tracing? No . . . Katherine could sense the devotion of the pioneers who had come this way before her, but no . . . not them. It was a connection she herself had to make. It was a tie to someone she couldn't name. Perhaps someone she did not know—perhaps would never see. But—yes—words would be the connection. Just as these letters marked on this skull linked her to those who had previously passed by, so her words would be a link. It became as plain to her as anything she had ever known.

Then as this one thought became imprinted in her mind, the incredible warmth began to ease and soften, until only a pleasantness remained.

"Katherine? I asked you a question," said Nathanial. "Are you there?" he chuckled.

Suddenly feeling weak, Katherine stood up and then sat back on a clump of grass. *A tie? A connection? To whom?* she wondered. And as she asked, the tie again began to forge, her heart to warm. There was someone. Someone, somehow. Katherine would write. She would keep a journal. She knew it was what she must do.

"Katherine," began Nathanial, now concerned. He took both her hands in his. "Are you all right?"

She took in a quick, deep breath, briefly opening her eyes wide to shift focus. *His hands and mine—how strange . . . it seems so . . . so natural and so . . . right. But it can't be right. . . .*

"I'm fine, Nathanial," she replied. "You've done nothing but help. I . . . I was just lost in thought, and, well, I felt a little dizzy."

"Mama!" called Isaac loudly. "Nathanial! Mama! Come quickly! The wagons are moving!"

A swell in the land prevented Katherine from seeing much of Isaac, but she did see his hand waving and his anxious face. Quickly, she pulled her hands away from Nathanial's.

"I'll go back with you," he said. "You lie down in the wagon while I harness the horses and get the wagon moving."

He swung Katherine up into his arms and began stepping through the dry patches of wild grass. "I'll carry you back."

"No, Nathanial," she said, laughing. "Put me down, please. I'm fine now. Truthfully."

"Are you sure?" he asked with a smile. "I'd very much like to carry you."

"I know you would." She chuckled. "Just let me down, though, please."

"All right," he responded, setting her on her feet. "But let me know if you feel dizzy again."

Katherine brushed off her skirt, and, glancing one last time at the marked skull, she walked with Nathanial to the wagon.

Five

"I'm clean!" insisted Gustavo in a voice somewhat muffled by the carpet. Still the cop snapped handcuffs around his wrists. Much larger and thicker than Katie had noticed them to be in movies, the cuffs looked invincible, as if they would still be around when everyone and everything else on earth had been annihilated by a nuclear bomb—even the cockroaches.

The same policeman neared Katie, and her eyes grew wide as another set of handcuffs dangled in her vision. They became larger than life, a symbol of incarceration and of the failure in life she had always feared was her destiny.

Katie's father had been in jail, at least once that she knew of. Katie had answered the telephone that night, about two years ago.

"I have a collect call from the Clark County jail in Nevada. The call is from Steven McBride. Will you accept the charges?" an operator asked.

Katie closed her eyes. "Yes," she answered and then took in a deep breath and waited.

"Baby? It's your daddy. I'm in a little fix here and need some help. Can I talk to your mom?"

Katie glanced over at her mother before she answered. Lying flat on the couch, she held a bottle of something toxic in one hand and the TV remote in the other. On the TV screen, the host of a game show peered at one of the three remaining contestants and asked, "After falling off a wall, which nursery rhyme character did all the king's men try to put together again?"

"Humpty Dumpty," quickly responded the contestant.

Katie's mother, lifting her bottle to her mouth, said weakly, "Humpty Dumpty. I knew that." Then she took a long drink.

"Just a minute," Katie responded finally. She took the telephone to her mother.

"Phone's for you."

"I don't . . . I just don't . . . ," Mrs. McBride mumbled, waving her hand with the remote in the air. "Who is it?"

"I don't know," Katie lied. "It's for you."

"Okay, okay." Dropping the remote to the wood floor, Katie's mother clumsily grabbed the phone.

"Hello? Who is it?"

"Steve?" Her voice grew louder and angry. "Steve? Steve?" It seemed that it was all she could do to repeat his name again and again, each time louder.

Katie could hear her dad's voice trying to get through to her mother.

"What do you want?" Mrs. McBride asked finally, a strange shrillness in her voice.

"Our final question," announced the host on TV, her glasses gleaming with stage lights. "Contestants, what sitcom featuring Ron Howard and Henry Winkler ran for ten years and became number one in American television in 1976?"

Happy Days. Katie knew the answer. Her mother knew it, too; she watched the reruns all the time. Mrs. McBride had stopped paying attention to the game show, though.

"What have you done this time?" asked Katie's mother, obviously disgusted with her ex-husband's request for five hundred dollars to post bail. "Have you robbed a bank?" She laughed scornfully.

"No, of course not. It's all a misunderstanding," he explained. "I'm here in Vegas, you know. The guy next to me was using magnets to loosen the slots, and they thought for some reason that I was in on it with him. I don't know the loser from Adam. I'm telling you the truth this time. I can clear this up tomorrow, honey. But I need bail today."

"Sure, Steve. Sure, you'll clear it up. Just do your fast-talkin' like you always do. But this is your garbage, Steve, so pick up a shovel and dig yourself out. Even if I had the money—which I don't—I wouldn't give it to you."

"They'll accept a credit card."

"A credit card!" yelled out Katie's mother. "How in the heck do you think I could make payments on a credit card? I don't have a card to my name. In eight years you haven't sent me a dime!"

"But, honey, you don't understand. I just haven't—"

"Oh, go to—!" Mrs. McBride ended the conversation with a string of expletives before flinging the phone across the room. And then she cried, on and off, on and off. For hours probably.

Having escaped the house to find fresh air and a change of scenery, Katie didn't know exactly how long her mother cried.

How ironic. The more Katie hated being like her parents, the more like them she became. The officer clamped the handcuffs first around one of Katie's wrists and then around the other. They felt cold and heavy.

"I just got here, you know," Katie said to the cop. "I didn't do any drugs. To tell you the truth, I never have."

"That pipe and lighter over there on the couch where you were sitting say differently, young lady." His voice was deep and unyielding. "That's constructive possession, a class 'A' misdemeanor."

"I promise. I've never had drugs in my life."

The officer stopped for just a moment and looked Katie squarely in the face. "What are you doing here then?" he finally asked.

It was obviously only a question for thought, though,

because he didn't wait for an answer. Within a few seconds the policeman had pulled both Katie and Gustavo off the floor and directed them to move forward.

Katie looked around. They were all walking toward the door, like zombies returning to their graves in an old black and white horror show, the living dead shuffling and moaning, their eyes hollow, their faces drained. The hundred-dollar girl marched out slowly, tears running down the Neiman-Marcus blush on her cheeks, while Melissa's feet, supported by a police officer, dragged along the carpet. Sam scratched at his face while he walked. *We're zombies. And we're all dead,* thought Katie.

Out the door, bright red and white lights flashed, revolving against their faces from the tops of at least six police cars parked right in the yard; there was no lawn to worry about, just weeds and dirt. Walkie-talkies sounded sporadically, seemingly from everywhere at once. Did the sound bounce off the bushes and the trees, or were there police hidden in the foliage, listening and responding to some faraway, monotone voice in their handsets?

The woman with the dark rings under her eyes turned to look at Gustavo before an officer guided her head under the roof of his car and into the backseat. Two younger men from the party sat in the backseat with her.

"*¡Gustavito! No te preocupes. ¡Los llamo después!*" the woman called out.

"My dad's friend," explained Gustavo. "She hangs around a lot."

Katie tried wiggling her wrists around to see if she could maneuver them out of the handcuffs. There was no wiggle room. "Where's your dad?" she asked Gustavo.

"He's out of town—a business deal."

"Okay, that's enough talk. Get in the car," ordered the police officer, looming over them. He must have been at least six foot four, and he had the shoulders of an offensive lineman.

Katie was sure the cop had never sat in the backseat of his own car. If he had, he would be stuck there still. Even Gustavo, who was only about five foot nine, had to scrunch up his knees almost to his chest. It was a sardine can. And they—Katie, Gustavo, and Sam—were the sardines. Katie had never been so glad she wasn't overweight.

With the last door shut, the officer lifted his walkie-talkie and spoke into it. What he said, though, Katie couldn't quite make out through the silence of the glass. It was probably something like, "Moving the losers in now. Have their cages ready. Roger that. Over and out."

As the policeman maneuvered the car back onto the road, Katie, looking out her side window, saw Stephen. He still stood on the grass, cigarette in hand. Noticing Katie's face in the window, he lifted his cigarette in a halfhearted good-bye. Then they sped off—quietly, though—the red and white lights still swirling from the cars in front and in back of them. Katie was a little disappointed that the sirens weren't blaring; they always did in the movies.

Right next to the glass window separating them from the front seat hung a computer printer. Katie sat forward and peered through the glass. A laptop was hooked into the seat, right at the cop's fingertips. What a joke! Katie didn't know how many times she had to tell one of her teachers that she really didn't have a computer at home. And here every police car had a built-in laptop and printer. *Oh, well. What does it matter? I'll be in jail for the rest of my life anyway.*

Before Katie and her friends had scrunched into the back-seat, the officer had asked if any one of them felt nauseated. They had all said no. Now, though, Sam grabbed his stomach and dry-heaved.

Gustavo knocked on the glass. "He's gonna throw up."

The policeman in the passenger seat turned his face toward the glass. It was like the magnified face of a zookeeper struggling to understand the animals.

"He's gonna throw up!" Gustavo repeated.

Slowing down quickly, the car pulled to the side of the road and stopped. Katie lifted the door handle, just to see if it might work, but no such luck. There would be no escaping from that car. Especially with handcuffs on.

Opening Sam's door, the offensive lineman told him to swing his legs out and lean his head away from the car. And then Sam threw up—and threw up twice more. It spread into the ditch of someone's sidewalk. Backing up so that the vomit wouldn't splatter on his uniform, the cop waited. Katie, from her vantage point, could see the officer from only his loaded belt down. She smiled. *It would be a shame*, thought Katie, *if the taser gun, walkie-talkie, magazines, keys, cell phone, and revolver, all hanging on his belt, were to become smothered in vomit.*

It didn't happen, though. Sam pulled his body back into the car, and the officer returned to his driver's seat clean.

The red and white lights continued to spin silently as the police cars parked near the back entrance of the station. Inside, Katie saw what she had never seen in a TV police station: a dilapidated dungeon. Monochrome yellow concrete from floor to wall to ceiling, the dingy holding area reeked of a disgusting odor that defied identification.

"I'll take your watch and earrings—and your ring. Remove your shoes and belt too," ordered a lady in a uniform. She dropped Katie's things in a large plastic bag, taped it shut, and stuck a numbered label on it. "You'll get them back when you leave," she added.

You mean if *I leave*, thought Katie.

The lady sat down at a computer, her shoes flat against the scratched yellow concrete. Rarely looking at Katie, the lady's eyes faced her computer monitor, which was jammed into a scratched yellow corner. "Name," the nameless face ordered.

"Katie, well . . . Katherine May McBride," she responded. Clasping her hands behind her neck, Katie closed her eyes and breathed in deeply before blowing the air out her mouth. *This must mean I'm being booked.*

"Address, please. Parents' names? School? Age?" There was no end to the woman's questions.

To the left of Katie, eight guys from the party had been

moved into a line, Gustavo and Sam being the only ones she knew. Wow, his face! Sam's face—and arms, chest, and stomach—were covered with blood; he had scratched himself raw. His face was the worst. Having heard that you can itch like crazy on meth, Katie never imagined it could be that bad.

"I'm clean," Katie heard Gustavo tell the officer who was attending him. "I've been clean for two weeks now," he added.

"You don't look too well for being clean," the officer responded as he checked Gustavo's eyes. "Maybe you should see a doctor."

Another cop, doing a search on one of the other guys, found a pipe in a back pocket. "These aren't my pants!" the boy explained. "I . . . I borrowed them from a friend," he added as he scratched down the length of his left leg. But the cop, with plastic-gloved fingers, still placed the pipe in a bag, and another policeman marked it.

"No, no! No!" It was a young-looking kid screaming at the back of the line. Suddenly there was a knife in his hand, and he was slicing it through the air to the rear of his jeans. Moving faster than Katie thought anyone could, three police officers, including the offensive lineman, surrounded the boy, and one of them took control of his knife.

"No! It's not my butt!" yelled the boy. "I have to cut it off—it's someone else's!" No one laughed. There was a long slice through the pocket of his jeans that kept them all from laughing.

"You'll be okay. You're just confused." The linebacker talked softly for several minutes to the boy and calmed him.

He's just a kid, thought Katie.

"Okay," said the lady attending Katie, getting up as she spoke. "Now stand with your legs spread and your arms out to the side, please. I'll be doing a quick search."

Katie couldn't believe that the woman was actually patting her body, head to toe. *This is stupid. Does she think I have a switchblade hidden between my toes?*

"Is this legal?" asked Katie. "I know how to call the child abuse hotline, you know. I've done it before."

"I'll bet you have, princess. We're almost through here. Don't you worry."

Somehow Katie didn't believe the woman really thought of her with such kindness. The officer's hair—Katie assumed she was an officer; after all, she had a badge—was a ball of blah-brown mousse sticks and frizz, just like the nest of a mouse.

"We'll just check your stability," continued the lady. "Walk along this line, please."

Stepping quickly, Katie walked the line easily. "Does this mean I can go?"

"That's not for me to say," she answered. "Hold still while I look at your eyes."

"Then who's to say?" asked Katie.

The police lady failed to respond. "This way, please," she said upon finishing her examination. She motioned Katie to walk in front of her.

"Wait a minute," said Katie, stopping in her tracks. "I get one phone call before you lock me up. I've seen it in lots of movies."

"Yes, dear. But we'll be making that phone call for you," her opaque pink–lipsticked lips answered. "We'll be calling your mother."

Katie laughed. "Good luck! She won't answer. She's bombed. She was totally passed out when I left her tonight."

As the officer escorted Katie down a corridor to an aisle of small cells, Katie noticed a man being led to the end of the aisle. His gait was uneven and listless. What was left of his hair hung in tangled strips down the back of his torn jacket. As the last cell door opened and the prisoner was motioned inside, he turned his head and looked back at Katie. She would never forget his face. Though the man was not old, his face was chiseled with scars and drooping lines and seemed to barely cling to his skull. His prominent nose, beaked and porous, almost touched the top of his blistered lips. A silver hoop hung from a stretched ear lobe, the aperture in the lobe long and gaping. His eyes were terrifying. They were cold and opaque, like quartz marbles. With no transparency or depth, his eyes showed no connection to humanity or warmth of any kind.

The man turned into his cell, and Katie shivered.

The police officer with Katie opened a metal door and directed her into an extremely small cell, about one yard square. Then she closed the door and barred it shut. *More!* thought Katie. *More scratched yellow concrete.* Katie sat on a slab of it that jutted out from the cell wall, her sockless feet cold against the bare floor. She shut her eyes tight. It was all a dull, uncared for, ugly monochrome, just like her life. *Why can't I be like Brittany Bradford, the homecoming queen and president of the ecology club? Or like Kim? She has a 4.0. If I could just be a little like Sean Adamson. He might even like me then. Or Mrs. Maxwell. She's at least doing something good with her life. Even Patricia Samuels. I'd much rather be fat and too perfect than be me. Here I am imprisoned just like the man with the cold, marble eyes. Does that mean I'm like him deep down inside?* Katie shivered again.

For over an hour, more like two, she sat and waited. The man in the cell at the end of the row began moaning. At first it was only faint, but later his moans became louder and with more lament. Several times Katie became startled by sudden outbursts, and she found herself flinching at the smallest noise.

Finally, the door opened. Standing there in front of her, all six foot four of him, was the cop who'd handcuffed her.

"I talked with your mother," he said, his arms folded across his chest. "She doesn't seem to be feeling well enough to pick you up, so I'll be taking you home.

"Your things," he said as he picked up her personal-item bag from outside the cell and held it out to her.

"I'm free to go?" asked Katie, skeptical.

"That's right," answered the policeman. "You're going home."

Home. I don't have a home; I have a house—an old, deteriorating house. And no one is really there.

"Here or there, it's all the same," she said to him. Katie put her shoes on and clasped her watch around her wrist. Dropping her earrings into her pocket, she decided not to bother with her belt either and slung it around her neck. Only her ring was left. Carefully, she slipped it over her finger and centered the dark stone.

Once again in the backseat of his car, this time alone, Katie tilted her head back and rested it against the seat until they arrived at her house. She looked at her watch. It was three o'clock in the morning.

"When I'm working and the day's tough," said the officer as he opened the door and waited for her to get out, "all that gets me by is thinking of getting home to my wife and my babies."

And just why is he telling me this? thought Katie. But she said nothing.

"If you were one of my daughters," the cop continued, "I'd tell you one thing."

"What would that be?" asked Katie, too tired to think of something clever to say.

"I'd tell you to decide what kind of person you want to be in life and then do whatever it takes to get there. You have to decide now, though. Or you'll go whatever direction the wind blows. I see it all the time."

For a split second, Katie saw the face of the marble-eyed prisoner. She blinked her own eyes tightly to shut out the image.

"So am I charged with anything?" asked Katie.

"No, you're clean—as clean as my patrol car," answered the officer as he shut the shiny backseat door and turned to go.

How clean can that be? For every druggie or drunk who managed to vomit outside of the car, Katie imagined there must be at least one or two who vomited inside.

"Thanks for the advice," she said, surprised at the sincerity in her voice. Then walking up the weedy rock path to her front door, Katie wondered why she hadn't been charged with constructive possession. Did this cop have something to do with it? Katie turned back around, but the police car was already halfway down the street.

Six

June 20, 1848

Dear Someone,

I feel I must write an account of my journey so that you might read it. I know not who you are or the purpose. I do know, however, that our lives will someday connect through this writing.

Tomorrow we are to reach Chimney Rock. We watch its tall spire grow ever taller and more magnificent as we draw closer. While the rays of the morning sun light upon it, I cannot help but be reminded of the majestic spire of the holy temple we left behind us in Nauvoo, or the City of Joseph. You should have seen our city! Such a picture of orderliness, beauty, and general contentment shall perhaps never be again. There my Michael and I found much happiness before he passed away. I must say, however, that even as tears slipped from my eyes when I turned to view the temple and our lovely city one more time before crossing the Mississippi, the Spirit of the Lord calmed my soul and spoke to me of peace and great hope. I and many of us were blessed to receive the Holy Anointings in that temple before we left, and I feel sure that the power of God will now rest upon us, his servants.

It is hard, though, without Michael. But the Lord is with me and with Isaac, and I know He shall prepare the way before us.

Here, Katherine finished. After carefully wiping the tip of her pen clean, she stopped up the ink bottle and closed her journal, the journal her mother had given her for her sixteenth birthday, eleven years ago tomorrow. Six months later her mother passed away. Katherine placed the journal in its box, also a gift from her mother, though a handed-down gift. The box had belonged to Katherine's Grandmother Devonshire. Ornately decorated with gold, the box had been used for jewelry. Katherine's mother had said that Grandmother Devonshire had called it "the garden box."

Even here in this wilderness—even here, though they cooked by campfire and slept on the boards of a wagon, if her mother were here, she would have done as she always did. She would've woken Katherine in the morning before dawn, the joyous look on her face felt more than seen. "Surprise!" she would exclaim. "It's your birthday, and you must come see the sunrise because the dawn is just for you today!" She would kiss her cheek and take her hand to lead her. Tomorrow, though, there would be no back porch from which to watch the sunrise. Instead, her mother would have led her to sit with her upon the wagon edge, their feet dangling in the cool night air. There they would've waited, with her mother's arm around Katherine to keep her warm, the smell of slow-sizzling bacon and her mother's special berry corncake circling them until the dark began to be less dark and then to lighten as the sun appeared over the east butte. "There it is, Katherine, dear. Happy, happy birthday. It's just for you."

Katherine knew the sunrise tomorrow would be for her, for her mother had always told her so. *If only she were here . . . . Perhaps if I will it hard enough, she will awaken me before the dawn. Perhaps I will feel her awakening me.*

"Katie, dear, there you are! That's enough writin' for now, for sure," declared Maddie. Thrust through the wagon curtains, her round face appeared isolated from the rest of her body and, in fact, took on a floating, moonlike appearance, lit as it was by the glow of Katherine's candle. "Come, dear! John is warmin' up his harmonica, and it appears Mr. Brighton has run to fetch his fiddle. Hurry, now, and we'll find a warm place by the fire."

For a moment Katherine wondered if Nathanial might be at the dance. She smiled and reached to take Maddie's waiting hand to help her down from the wagon.

"There's that smile now—the brightest smile east of the Foyle river, it is. Never want to lose that, now, do you, Katie?"

"No, Madeline, I don't," responded Katherine as she jumped to the ground. "Then I'd surely be lost in this wilderness."

A light breeze blew gently at their backs as Katherine, Madeline, and Isaac made their way by the light of the moon to the campfire. The evening was cool, as evenings on the prairie often were, welcome relief from the relentless heat of the day. The darkening of the colors of the earth and skies seemed at times to close in on Katherine, though, weighting her with weariness and collapsing her determination. But she wasn't the only one. Katherine had noticed the footsteps of her fellow travelers slowed immensely, and the optimism fell from their faces as the night wore on. Grumblers, rarely heard during the day's march, murmured behind wagons and at the far edges of the campfire to anyone who would listen. Nightly festivities were the antidote, and Katherine didn't know of anyone who didn't look forward to them.

"Hear that, Mother?" exclaimed Isaac excitedly. "Sounds like someone's brought fireworks!"

"Now, and wouldn't that be nice, child," said Maddie. "Even our blessed Saint Patrick would be dancin' a mighty jig from his throne in heaven to see a grand display of fire light up the night sky of this lonesome plain."

"I am loathe to disappoint the both of you," replied Katherine. "But I believe the explosions we hear are but the popping of some extra dry buffalo chips in the campfire ahead."

"That and nothin' more?" asked Maddie incredulously.

"That and nothing more," repeated Katherine with finality.

Sam Brighton, though, soon livened the night enough. Lifting his fiddle up to his chin and then tapping a rhythm with his toe to a flat rock, Sam's face spread open in a wide grin, and he began to play. The notes, dropping to a melancholy contralto and up again to a floating treble, danced through the darkness, fast and free.

Maddie sighed contentedly as she rested her chin in the palm of her hand, her elbow planted firmly on her wide knee. "Ah . . ." she exclaimed. "'Tis his own heart that is surely in it. Not even in Dublin would I hear fiddlin' that reaches inside as does his."

As Maddie concluded, young John Jamison, stepped sprightly up next to Mr. Brighton, his harmonica nimble in his fingers as he waited for the right moment to join in.

"There ya go, Johnny!" called someone from the opposite side of the campfire. "That'll make up for this mornin' when you missed the snake and blasted a hole in your canteen instead!"

"Good thing that snake weren't a-thirsty," added another voice. "If'n that snake'd come for your canteen instead of hightailin' it out'a there, you might not be alive right now to play that harmonica o' yours, now would ya?"

"No," laughed John, his smile just as big and wide as Sam's. "No, sir, Brother Pettigrew," he continued. "And then you, sir, would have to play this here harmonica in my place, and the rest of you would all be wishin' you'd have been bit by that snake instead of havin' to be here listenin'!" And with that John blew into his harmonica loud and strong, his notes weaving in and out of the notes of Mr. Brighton's fiddle and sometimes chorusing with them.

Feeling a soft tap on her shoulder, Katherine thought it was Nathanial. She smiled and turned, but it was not him. The disappointment she felt surprised her.

"Shall we dance, Katherine?" It was Amos Taggart, a

politician by trade. Unmarried, he seemed to be regarded by the other single women as the prize catch of the wagon company.

"Aye, as I was telling you," said Maddie quickly and as if she had been chatting with Katherine all along, "me father ran a wee little feed store just north of Dublin, and I'm very airy about it, but I believe—"

"Madeline," interrupted Katherine. "Amos wishes to dance, and I believe that by doing so I shall warm myself. May we finish this account of your father's store afterward?"

"Hmph," grunted Maddie. "I don't mind at all, to be sure. But one wee dance, will you please, or the tale may fail me."

"Just one dance it is then, Madeline. Brother Taggart?"

After bowing slightly to Maddie, Amos squared his elbow for Katherine to take his arm, and they began two-stepping in front of the fire. Smoke and kicked-up dust soon blocked Maddie's view of them.

"He's so full of himself and all that he's famous for it's just a wonder he doesn't float entirely up into the night sky to bang his fine head on some star."

"What's that, Maddie? What does that mean?" commented Isaac, who sat next to her, his head comfortable against her soft shoulder.

"Never you mind, Isaac, dear. Never you mind. Just remember to always keep your wee feet planted on the ground. Only keep them planted deep in that good earth the Lord gave us."

"Don't worry, Maddie. I've walked and walked and walked and walked—and walked. Clear from Nauvoo, almost to Chimney Rock. My feet are definitely on the ground."

Maddie chuckled. "Good for you, lad, good for you. Faith'n I do believe some merrymaking would warm this old body—and your little-boy body as well. How about a bit of dancin', then?"

"Don't mind if I do!" responded Isaac with a laugh and a polite nod of his head. "Do you know how to dance?"

"'Do I know how to dance,' says he! Oh, me boy, they wouldn't call me the Londonderry Bird for no reason, now would they?"

And then she began to dance. How Madeline McFarland was able to move her feet so fast and in seemingly every direction at once while they carried the weight and size of an extra wide and bulky tree stump is anyone's guess. His legs fumbling and fluttering in an attempt to stay with her, Isaac seemed much like a life-size ragdoll with cotton hands attached securely to the hands of his dance partner.

"What's troublin' you now, me Katie?" asked Madeline with great pants and gusts of breath as the dance ended and Isaac walked back with her to their previous position, where Katherine stood waiting for them. "You look, darlin', as if your crop o' potatoes had just been hit by a blight!"

"It's not what I've lost, Maddie. It's what I can't quite find," replied Katherine, her voice distant, the flames of the campfire intensified in her eyes.

"Let me see now," reasoned Madeline. "'Tis something she can't find, but she's not lost it either. A riddle much too complex for this wee brain o' mine. Make it clear for me now, Katie, dear."

Katherine turned her gaze from the fire and looked at Madeline. "When we were dancing, Madeline, Amos stepped on my toe, and then I stepped on his. I lost my balance and would have fallen into a giant sagebrush if he hadn't caught me. But that's not it. You see, we started laughing. We laughed so hard Amos could hardly catch his breath, and neither could I.

"And that's when I felt it. I felt a sudden gravity come over me and burn within me so strongly that it almost made me cry. I felt as if I had no right to laugh and be merry—as if my laughter shouldn't be while someone important to me is in despair. 'Brother Taggart,' I said. 'Would you mind terribly if we ended this dance?' He must think horribly of me now, but I couldn't dance anymore. It's a feeling that has been growing ever stronger for many days now. What am I to do, Maddie? How can I help when I know not even who it is I must assist? And Amos, Maddie. He'll think I loathe his company. Why, he might never speak to me again!"

"All I know, Katie dear, is that when God wants a person to

know a certain thing, he lets them know it—then, and not a moment sooner, to be sure. And it's no use tryin' to hurry Himself up," advised Maddie.

"It's your man there that I'm after worryin' about," she continued. "And what a grand blessing 'twould be, darlin', if the man ne'er spoke to you again! He has quite a wish for you, he does. I'm after tellin' you, though, Katie, that these bones o' mine aren't creakin' on this good earth this long for nothin'. I've me lessons learned about men, Katherine. And you'll be believin' me when I tell you that boy is not what I would be callin' a gentleman."

"Maddie, of course I'm not interested in Brother Taggart. How could I be? No one compares to Michael," responded Katherine. "But, Maddie, how can you say such a thing about Amos? In Nauvoo, he was very highly respected, a devout elder in the church. And you should have heard him speak at town meetings. He spoke so eloquently and with such life that it would almost take your breath away."

"And your breath away, indeed! Only like the devil himself! 'Twas all blarney and bonnyclabber—tasty, mind you, but comin' from the sour milk, nevertheless. If you're after findin' a true gentleman, Katie, dear, you better be lookin' elsewhere. Me advice is good riddance t'that one!"

Katherine's eyes grew wide at the force of Maddie's accusations, but she said nothing.

"Speakin' o' lookin' elsewhere, me girl, to yer left you'll see as fine a man you'll ever come upon, and the man's headed our direction, he is. That there's the type o' man you need."

Katherine turned to look. "Nathanial?" she whispered. "Yes, he is a fine man, but what about Michael? Why, Maddie, it's only been a little over a year—and, besides, I doubt that I'll ever be interested in marrying again! You surprise me, Maddie. You—just like Michael's mother—and wanting me to forget him!"

"Up here for thinkin', Katie," said Madeline as she pointed to her own head, "and down here for dancin'." Curving her toes upward, she pointed to her stubby feet. "You wouldn't go astray if you thought o' the future," whispered Maddie. "I don't want you to forget me Michael, girl, just live yer life happy without him. You know yerself that bones grow old, Katie, dear. Let someone else's bones grow old wi' ye."

"Good evenin', ladies!" said Nathanial as he grew close. "May I join you, or is this a private meeting? You two seem very secretive. You aren't devisin' plans to overthrow the government, are you?"

"Oh, that's grand, me boy!" Madeline laughed. "Are you after thinkin' I'm away in the head now? I'd have t'be entirely flootered to think I could manage more than the direction o' me own two shoes, now wouldn't I? And right this moment I do believe I'll be pointin' me shoes back to the wagon and take the weight off me legs. The extra potato in the pot does best to jump out, I always say."

"You are no extra potato, Maddie," said Katherine, chuckling. "But if you are going back to the wagon, I'd better leave with you and take Isaac. He must be exhausted."

"Don't worry yourself, me girl. I'll take the boy wi' me, I will," responded Maddie as she shipped off in Isaac's direction. "Take care!"

Most of those who had collected around the fire had gone or were gathering their blankets to leave. Sam and John played on, though, as if they planned to do so through the night, and a few couples still danced.

Katherine walked with Nathanial to the dying campfire and watched him drop two heavy logs onto the fire and hunch down to stir the coals. He closed his eyes for a moment, and Katherine noticed the smoothness of his eyelids and the curve of his long dark eyelashes as they fell against his skin. It became a picture in her mind that returned to her often. And always when it did, she would shake her head and wonder why the picture stayed.

"Shall we dance?" asked Nathanial as he stood up.

"Yes," answered Katherine. "Yes, we shall."

With the melody now hushed and lyrical, Nathanial took

Katherine's hand in his and rested his other hand lightly at her waist. It felt to Katherine like his hands had always belonged there. She looked up and searched his eyes to figure out why.

"I'm not much of a dancer, you know," he said as they moved in a slow, four-beat pattern.

"That's all right," Katherine answered. "My father always said that good dancers are easy to come by, but a man who really listens to the music is rare."

"And how do you know if a man really listens to the music?"

Katherine wasn't quite sure what to say. "I don't know," she finally answered. "But I think you can tell by his kindness."

His kindness. Her thoughts circled with a new awareness, and she looked intently at Nathanial. *Yes, Nathanial is certainly kind—he's one of the kindest men I've ever known.*

Leading Katherine to the shadowy outskirts of the circle around the fire, Nathanial slowed his steps and finally stopped altogether. "Katherine," he said. "Do you remember the night you and Michael became engaged? He said he was too shy to look at you in person, and so he sat back to back with you on a log out by the river. And then he asked you to marry him."

"I remember, Nathanial. Of course I remember."

"That night, Katherine, was the most difficult of my life." Nathanial cleared his throat and looked off into the distance. Then he looked directly back at Katherine. "I have to tell you this, Katherine. I . . . well, I loved you then, Kate. I loved you very much then—and I still do."

Katherine's heart jumped. "I—"

"Wait, please. I have to finish," Nathanial interrupted as he took her hands in his. "I couldn't tell you—and, of course, I couldn't tell Michael. He loved you first. And he was my best friend. But now, Katherine, I need to know." His hands gripped hers more tightly. "I need to know if you can ever forget Michael enough to think of me. I need to know, Kate, well . . . if you might ever love me. Because . . . because I've loved you for so long—for years now, Katherine, and I can't stand being around you not knowing if I can ever mean anything to you."

Katherine's eyes intensified as she looked into his, and her heart warmed. She had to stop herself from reaching out to touch his face. Then, even as she felt that for some crazy reason they belonged to each other—even as Katherine felt that she actually might love Nathanial right now and very much—she found herself shaking her head.

"No, Nathanial. No. It can't be. It just can't be."

Nathanial looked down at her hands, which he held in his, his eyelashes again sweeping his skin. He remained quiet for some time as Katherine stood mute, her eyes shifting away and then back to him again.

"All right, then, Katherine. At least now I know. Whenever you need me, I'll be there for you. But I won't be around so much, Kate. I just can't."

Then he walked her to her wagon.

Katherine did not crawl inside the wagon to sleep just yet. Upturning a metal pail, she sat on top and rubbed her fingers over her eyes and through her hair. It was all so strange.

She had always loved Michael, from the first moment she saw him. Traveling house to house with his cart, selling fruit from his orchard, Michael knocked on her family's farmhouse door. Just eighteen years old at the time, Katherine was so taken by him as she answered the door that she forgot to say hello. He at first assumed that she was unable to speak. Katherine had promised him later that she would always love him—always. If he had lived, they would have received the holy sealing. For eternity.

And now what about Nathanial? As she thought of him, her heart warmed and began to swell. The overwhelming feeling became stronger each second. *This is wrong! It's a silly emotion that doesn't mean anything.* Katherine tried to block out the feeling. She closed her eyes tightly, pushed on her chest, and took a deep, relaxing breath. But the sensation remained and even grew stronger. So much stronger that it hurt.

Oh, Lord. Remove this from me. What's wrong with me? Can't I be faithful to Michael? Take this feeling away, Lord—and let me love Michael.

But the feeling would not go, as much as Katherine tried to rid herself of it. Climbing up into the wagon, she lay down at Isaac's side, and the strange feeling soon lost itself in her sleep.

Seven

Katie rolled over to her side, opened her eyes narrowly, and then let them drop slowly. Groaning, she rolled to the other side and hugged her pillow tightly. Though her room had grown brighter with the new day, Katie wasn't ready for it yet. She wasn't ever ready for it.

This morning, though, was especially difficult. Images of needles, of Gustavo's hazy front room, and then of stark, bright police station lights pulsating over her filled Katie's mind. Did it all really happen? Or was it a dream? Her eyelids dropped closed once again to shut out the unwelcome images, but her mind refused to shut down. Contrarily, it began to quicken as she reviewed and analyzed a few particularly stupid or embarrassing moments. Soon the images became too focused and too detailed to ignore. And then much as the sleeping passenger in a run-away locomotive awakens suddenly to a desperate reality, Katie was at once fully awake. It was all real.

Well, at least I didn't do any drugs, Katie reasoned. And since she was clean, they didn't arrest her like they did the others. *Things aren't all bad then,* thought Katie as she let her head sink back into her pillow. It could have turned out much worse. I could have taken the meth, and I could have been charged. And next time . . . next time . . . But Katie didn't know what, if anything, she would do differently next time.

She glanced at the clock at her bedside: 7:05 a.m. It was

time for school, and today was the last day. It might even be fun at school today—in a stupid sort of way. Maybe she could pull herself out of bed, get dressed, and then just lie back down under the covers for a while, just until the bus was almost here. Then again, maybe not. Katie shut both eyes tightly, relaxed into her pillow, and purposely let her mind drift. Sleep was so good, and her bed was safe, and her head had begun to ache. It was all too much. Way too much. After all, she was only a young teenager. Way too young to deal with a drunken, depressed mother, with the school superintendent, with friends that weren't really friends, and with scary cops. *Why did I have to stay at Gustavo's party last night? Why? I should have turned back around as soon as I walked in the door. Why can't I ever do anything right?* It was all way too much. *And today is my birthday*, remembered Katie. *Happy birthday to me.* She let the tears slip from her eyelids; no one could see her now. *Well*, she almost laughed, *it's not like anyone would care if they did see me.*

After some time, Katie slept. The bus braked and slowed as it passed her house, but Katie neither saw nor heard it.

"Happy birthday, Katie," exclaimed her mother late that afternoon from the depths of her sunken scarlet armchair. Her mother's voice was weak but not without feeling. Her left hand lay limp in her lap along with a wallet, her right hand loosely surrounding an empty glass on the side table. Katie, having treated herself to a birthday Coke at the convenience store on the corner, entered the house and stopped to listen. Her mother sounded almost sober.

"Here, this is for you." Katie's mother reached into her wallet and took out a twenty-dollar bill. Her hand was steady as she held it out for Katie. "I never did get to the store to buy you a present, but you'll probably like something you've picked out for yourself better anyway. I know it's not much, but . . . ." Here her mother's voice faded, and her gaze shifted from Katie to the empty glass on the table.

Katie understood. Her mother was giving Katie the last of her liquor money stash. Perhaps her mother would have to go dry now for a few days until the next check came in the mail.

"Heck," said her mother. "Maybe you can buy a new CD or a movie. Or maybe a new pair of jeans. Is there something you need for that trek you're takin' tomorrow? We could run over to the store now."

Katie sat down on the corner of the old blue couch—the faded flower-print couch where she had sat years ago to open birthday gifts. Her father had sat in the scarlet armchair then, and her mother on the piano bench. They had all smiled. Katie thought she could remember the smiles.

"No," replied Katie. "I don't need anything for the trek. They gave me two pioneer dresses to wear, and I'm not allowed to take much else. Thanks for the money. I'll buy something when I get back."

Katie's mother looked down now at her hands as she held them together in her lap over the wallet. "I'm sorry, Katie," she said. "I'm sorry for . . . for everything. I haven't been . . . I really haven't been a good mother to you. We both know it." Then she looked up slowly from her hands and met Katie's gaze. "I just can't . . . I can't seem to make things go right."

Katie almost reached her hand out to touch her mother, the long-ago mother she remembered had loved her. She held her hand back, though. *What am I supposed to feel—to say? "It's okay, Mom. Who cares if you've wrecked the last six years of my life?" Or perhaps, "Oh, well! We all make mistakes!" No. It's not okay. It will never be okay.*

Katie stood up. "I need to get my stuff ready for tomorrow," she said.

"Need help?" asked Katie's mother, attempting to push herself up from the chair.

"No, I'm good. There's not much to do."

In her bedroom, Katie sat heavily at the side of her bed

and stared out the window. *Why me? Why is this my life? Was I just born no good? Is this my life because I deserve it?* Turning her eyes to the mountaintop and the expanse of blue that encased it, Katie's gaze continued upward across the sky as far as she could see. Then just in case some being way up there in the unknown might be listening, and with a sincere intensity Katie didn't know she was capable of, she whispered aloud: "Why?" The word echoed around the paint-chipped walls of the room, slid across the swinging, oval mirror, and then nestled inside the hollow places of the old armoire.

Katie waited a few moments, but no answer came. *Like I really expected someone to answer,* she thought. Opening her eyes wide to dry them, Katie then rubbed her fingers over her closed eyelids and glided her hands over her ears to pull her hair up and away from her face. She noticed quickly that her right earring was missing. They were her favorite earrings too!

Katie checked her bed and then began to search the floor. The wooden floorboards must have dated back to the origins of the house in the late 1800s: some boards bowed deep; others were splintered. Many creaked even at night while Katie slept. Cracked seams and rotted-out knots waited to catch and forever imprison any small thing Katie might drop. Her favorite earrings! Katie's heart felt sick to think her earring might now lie under those old boards.

As Katie looked across the room, she saw it. The earring lay on the floor in the corner of the room, right next to the wall. When she tried to pick it up, though, the earring slipped down the crack between the boards. *Murphy's law,* thought Katie. As she pried at the board, however, she found that it was not nailed down like all the others; indeed, Katie was able to lift it up easily with her hands. She peered down into the exposed blackness. There could be snakes down there. Or black widows. Maybe even light-deprived, slimy frogs turned albino. But Katie thought she could see the earring far down inside, and she didn't want to have to spend her birthday money on a new pair of earrings; she had already been counting on that money to buy music for the iPod she found. Taking a deep breath, she reached her hand in cautiously. There was the earring! Carefully catching hold of it, Katie felt something underneath. Some sort of box, perhaps.

After picking up the earring and quickly sliding it back in place on her ear, she looked back into the hole. There she could see a dim outline of something. Something that sparkled. Katie reached back inside and grasped the strange object. It really was a box! Turning it on its side so as to fit it through the opening, Katie lifted it out.

The box was small, probably only about six by four inches. What shone was a piece of one gold leaf, the only part of a trail of vines, roses, and leaves that wasn't blackened with tarnish. Opening the box, Katie lifted out a small, beaten book. More than time had marred it. Its edges were smashed, the binding hung in tatters, and the surface was severely scratched. The book almost appeared to have risen from the dead. Katie opened it with as little pressure from her fingertips as she could manage, perhaps the same as a surgeon might do as he pushes aside an artery to reach the heart. She was afraid the pages might crumble in her hands.

The date was written clearly on the first page: "June 20, 1848." No! It couldn't be! Katie read the date again. She read it three times more. This book is over one hundred fifty years old! She wondered immediately how much it might be worth.

"Dear Someone," Katie began reading. It appeared to be a diary. "Tomorrow we are to reach Chimney Rock," wrote the writer of the journal. *Chimney Rock? Where is that?* Nauvoo. Katie had heard of Nauvoo. Something to do with the Mormons. Katie knew that those who built her house were Mormons. And hadn't she been told that her house was over one hundred years old? The journal could have been hidden under the floorboards as the house was being built.

Katie read on. Michael was her husband and he died. And she really loved him. "But the Lord is with me and with Isaac, and I know He shall prepare the way before us," the author wrote. *Wow. How would it be to really believe in something like that? To believe that there was a God who is there for you, who takes care of you. How would it be?* Katie's heart felt empty in comparison and ached to believe in something as strongly.

After reading the page one more time, she smoothed it out and carefully closed the little book. That was enough for today; it had already given Katie much to think about. *I'll take it on the trek. It'll give me something to do when I'm bored.* Placing the book back in its box, Katie wrapped the box carefully in an old T-shirt and then placed it at the bottom of the bucket Pam Collins had given her to store her personal items on the trek.

Eight

The blare of Katie's alarm clock woke her. She automatically stretched her left arm over to slam the snooze button and opened her eyes just a slit to check the time. 6:00 a.m. Who in their right mind would get up at 6:00 a.m.? And then Katie remembered. This morning was the trek. And she had to be at the Mormon church on the corner at 6:30 a.m. sharp. If she didn't do the trek—the full two weeks of it—she would have to spend time locked up. How long she would be locked up, Katie didn't know. She couldn't count on good behavior to shorten the sentence; that was something Katie knew she wasn't good at, especially if it were forced upon her. This trek had to be the better choice.

Groaning, Katie rolled out of bed and trudged into the bathroom—the only working bathroom in the house. An empty bottle of scotch glared at her from the chipped windowsill.

"Yep," mumbled Katie aloud, seemingly talking to the empty bottle. "This is your house, isn't it, and no one else's. Well, if you don't mind, I need to share the bathroom with you this morning. I'm going on a trek."

Katie showered quickly and then pulled one of the pioneer dresses the detention officer had brought to her out of its bag. She couldn't believe it! Was she expected to wear all this stuff? Taking out first a faded blue cotton print skirt with a pinafore, Katie then pulled out a blue bonnet with ties, an obviously well-used, dingy white apron, an equally dingy button-down shirt, and last, and perhaps least, a pair of funny-looking, huge pantaloons.

"Am I going to be a clown or a pioneer?" grumbled Katie to herself. Remembering, however, that the contract she signed included a restriction that she wear pioneer dress, Katie put it all on and then walked to the old, full-length mirror in her bedroom.

"Well, this is a blast from the past," joked Katie. As she stared into the old oval mirror, however, her mind grew quiet. She seemed to recognize her reflection. It reminded her of something—a portrait she had seen once of an ancestor perhaps. Try as she might, though, Katie could not quite remember. Something about the eyes together with the bonnet . . . the dark eyes and the faded blue bonnet. Katie reached out to touch the glass with her fingertips and then let them slide over the rough roses carved into its antique wooden frame. Of the entire hand-me-down house, complete with rusty hinges, rotting wooden floors, and leaks in the roof, this swinging oval mirror was the only relic Katie valued. She stepped back one step and stared again at this pioneer reflection of herself. Maybe it was an ancestor of her father's that she reminded herself of.

No more time for this. I can't be late. Grabbing her toothbrush, Katie threw it into the bucket of items she had packed the day before. She glanced momentarily at the iPod on her dresser, the one she had slipped in her backpack a week earlier. The rules on her list read, "Take absolutely nothing more than the items on this list. We do not have room for anything else. Your bucket will be checked before departure."

I doubt it, thought Katie. *The judge said there would be a hundred kids going on this trek. How would they ever be able to check all of the buckets?* Packing the iPod on top of the wrapped box containing the old journal, Katie pressed the lid of the bucket down tightly and walked out the door without bothering to say good-bye to her mother. The empty bottle in the bathroom told Katie that her mother would be totally out of it. Mrs. McBride must have found some scotch she had hidden somewhere around the house just for a rainy day. Katie wouldn't have been able to wake her even if she had tried.

In five minutes the church building was within Katie's view. Her memories of that particular building were not good ones. She had only been there twice that she could remember; her mother had taken her two Sundays in a row right after her father left. Katie's mother had told her then that she—her mother—was actually a member of that church. When Katie asked her why they had not attended previously, Katie's mother, after some thought, mumbled, "I didn't know if we belonged there."

"Do we belong there now?" Katie had asked.

"I don't know," was her mother's reply. "I'm hoping we do."

There was something about what her mother said that the ten-year-old Katie liked. Hoping was good. Hoping held a desire and maybe even a hint of a promise that things would get better.

Katie felt something good there that first week at church, and she thought her mother did as well. The second Sunday, though, something happened. Katie often wore her hair in two long braids back then, and during Sunday school, the elastic on one of her braids broke. As Katie was in the bathroom redoing her hair into one braid to fit the one remaining elastic, a woman pushed the door open partway to enter and then stopped there at the door to speak with someone Katie could not see or hear very well who stood outside the door.

"I think so too," said the lady holding the bathroom door open. "Someone should talk with her."

Then the other person spoke. Most of what she said Katie could not hear well enough to understand, but Katie's hand stopped braiding, and her heart began to pound when she heard her mother's name.

"I can't even stand to get close to her." It was the first woman speaking now. "She positively reeks of smoke. And—" here the woman hushed her voice—"I'm sure I smelled alcohol on her

breath when I said hello to her before church started this morning."

Katie thought she heard the woman she could not see say
something about the bishop, and then the conversation ended
and the door opened wider as the first woman made her way
into the bathroom. Katie thought of several choices. She could
dive quickly into the bathroom stall and hope the woman would
not notice her, she could stay planted in front of the mirror
and pretend she hadn't heard anything, or she could confront
the woman and ask her bluntly why she would say such mean
things about her mother. Katie was not defenseless now nor had
she been at ten years of age; she chose silent confrontation.

As the woman entered, Katie slowly turned from the
mirror to face her and stared at her straight in the eyes. Obviously shocked to see Katie standing there, the woman stopped
abruptly, the shoulder strap of her purse falling off her shoulder.
The woman turned to catch her purse and then looked back at
her. Katie only continued to stare.

"I didn't mean . . ." started the woman. "I'm sorry, I . . ." And
then seemingly at a loss for words, the woman turned around
and left the bathroom.

Katie turned back to the mirror and began to cry.

After church Katie told her mother what had happened. She
regretted telling her, though, for months—and perhaps for
years—because Katie's mother never returned to church after
that. And the hope that Katie had so prized was gone for good.

And now Katie was back again at that same church. If her
mother wasn't sure if they belonged there six years ago, Katie
was positive they didn't belong there now.

"Just look at all those goody-goodies," said Katie to no one
as she stopped to take in the trek departure scene. Cars splattered randomly around the parking lot, teenagers and adults
in pioneer skirts, blue jeans, and cowboy hats stood or walked
around in small groups, some dangling their legs from truck
tailgates. Buckets just like hers were everywhere. Katie noticed
a few adults seated at or milling around a table set up at one

side of the building. She thought that might be check-in and headed in that direction.

"Here you are! Right on my list," announced one of the adults at the table after Katie had given him her name. *Well, of course I'm on your list, dork. Do prisoners get off the list for death row?* Katie tried to smile back at the man. Maybe he didn't know, though, that this was her sentence.

"You're assigned to cart number twenty-two, right over there to your left," said the man as he stretched out his arm and pointed. "But first swing your bucket up here on the table, and Sister Morrison will have a look-see at what you've packed. We need to make sure you're totally prepared, you know," added the man as he flashed a totally fake smile at Katie. *A look-see! What kind of stupid baby talk is that? And no one should be having a look-see at my personal things.*

"You don't need to check. I'm totally prepared with everything that was on the list," replied Katie as the bucket hung from her hands behind her back.

But then she felt her bucket being lifted up by someone behind her. "Everyone gets checked," said that someone as Katie let go of the bucket. It landed in the hands of the checker. And Katie, the checkee, could do nothing. Then as she turned to look at the woman who had grabbed the bucket, Katie recognized the short and wavy brown hair and the I-know-every-trick-in-the-book brown eyes. It was her social worker, Pam. Katie thought it best to pretend they didn't know each other, and evidently so did Pam—she said nothing more to Katie.

"What have we here?" said the first man again in what Katie thought to be imitation baby language. "An iPod? Now, Sister McBride, you must not have noticed that all such things are restricted from this trek! We want a true pioneer experience. Don't worry, though," the man said as he wrote her name on a piece of masking tape and stuck it to the iPod. "We'll get this right back to you as soon as the trek is over." Then he placed it in a huge box that was already half full of taped items. "You go have fun now. That way, remember? Cart twenty-two." And his arm again reached across the table and across the face of the checker lady seated next to him as he pointed the way Katie should go.

It's impolite to point, you know, thought Katie. Then she turned and walked slowly in the indicated direction.

As Katie neared a group centered around a blue pick-up truck, an adult in the group with a huge smile called out to her. "Hope you're lookin' for cart twenty-two! 'Cause that's us, and it'd be great to have you with us!"

Hmmm, wait till you know me, thought Katie. But she answered back semi-politely, "Yeah, that's my number."

"Well, get on over here, then," said the man. "I suppose you've checked in and had your bucket cleared and everything?"

"I've had it cleared," answered Katie, a little sauciness in her voice. "But I don't know if they've left me much in it."

"Welcome to the crowd," replied the man. "We're all going to be roughin' it big time."

"They took my bag of M&M's and my makeup too," said one of the two girls seated on the tailgate. She didn't seem very happy about it.

The tall boy with the cowboy hat standing near her added, "They wouldn't let me keep my camera. They said that some-one was assigned to take pictures of all the handcart families anyway. It's okay, though," he added, straightening his cowboy hat and looking in the direction of the man. "I figured they probably wouldn't let me take it."

Hmmm . . . thought Katie. She squinted her eyes and imag-ined the boy without his hat. *He's actually not bad looking, in a goody-goody sort of way.*

"Let's introduce ourselves, okay?" said the man in charge, smiling widely again. "I believe we're all here now. Maybe after we each say our names, we can tell about a hobby or something we really like to do." Then clearing his throat and straighten-ing out his neck, the man continued. "I'll start. I'm your pa for the trek, Brother Paul. And I looove to go four-wheeling. And so does my real family. Our kids are all grown up now, but we still go riding at least once each month."

"Now tell us *your* name," he said placing his hand on the shoulder of a short boy with glasses standing near him. "You already told me that you play Xbox quite a bit, but maybe there's something you like to do even better."

"My name is Zach," the boy said quietly as he gazed at an undefined point somewhere between Katie and the girl standing nearest her. "And, I don't know, I like math, I guess. It's my best subject in school."

You look the part, thought Katie. *You've got "nerd" written all over you.*

"Now I'll know where to go for help when I'm trying to crunch some numbers," said Brother Paul. "I never was very good at math," he chuckled. "Glad to have you with us. And what about you?" he asked, looking at the girl who had lost her M&M's and makeup.

"I'm Lindsay Cook. And I like dancing. I've been taking dance lessons for five years."

Katie's eyes moved down and then up again as she took in the thirty or forty extra pounds of weight that belonged to Lindsay. *How on earth can you move all that around to music?* thought Katie. *And I'm going to be with these people for two long weeks?*

"That's awesome, Lindsay, just awesome," commented Brother Paul.

Awesome, I guess! It's a miracle, that's what it is.

"Now my family already has two talents that I don't," continued Brother Paul, never letting go of that great big smile of his. Katie was beginning to think it was plastic and glued to his face. "Okay, next?" he said, looking at the other girl sitting on the tailgate next to—but not too close to—Lindsay. Katie didn't recognize her, but she could just bet the girl was a cheerleader. You could always tell a cheerleader.

"I'm Micah," she said, bubbling up her voice, straightening her back, and tilting her head just so as if there were a camera in front of her. "I'm really into cheer. It takes just about all my time."

I'll bet it does, thought Katie. *That and looking in the mirror.*

"Wow! A real cheerleader! What school do you cheer for?" asked Brother Paul.

Here Katie just about lost it because Micah jutted her elbow down, her hand clenched, and shot her arm up straight in the air in a show of victory as she proudly announced, "Brigham Mustangs!"

O-o-o-h, my heavens. Should I throw up now or later?

"Brigham High, you say," confirmed Brother Paul. "My kids have all gone to Washington High. Do you like it at Brigham?"

For an answer, Micah opened her eyes wide and nodded her head several times while she smiled.

"Well, none of you would ever want to see me try to do cheer, would they, Ma?" Brother Paul looked at the only grown-up woman in the group, who must have been his wife.

"No, I think not," she replied, smiling back at Brother Paul. She obviously liked him a lot. You could see it in the way she looked at him. And then as the next boy in the group began to speak, Katie looked back again at the woman. Katie was sure she knew her from somewhere.

"Morgan. That's an awesome name! I have a son named Morgan. He's married now. So what is it you like to do most?" asked Brother Paul.

Morgan drummed the tin cup hanging from his belt loop and, narrowing his eyes, looked first to the left, then to the right, and tapped his fingers to his lips. "I don't know. I like lots of things. But I'm sure all of you do. I guess I'll say hiking. My dad and I go hiking a lot in the mountains."

"I know your dad," said Brother Paul. "There's not a better man around. Isn't he on this trek?"

"Yeah, my mom, too. They're on cart eight," replied Morgan as he straightened his cowboy hat once again. He was obviously the oldest teen in the group, looking around seventeen or eighteen years old.

"Awesome!" exclaimed Brother Paul.

I didn't think it was possible to use the word awesome *so many times in a five-minute period. It shouldn't even be legal,* thought Katie.

"Well, two more to go. Tell us your name," Brother Paul directed his comment to a freckled girl wearing a purple pinafore who stood at a slight distance from the rest of the group. "I already know it, but the others don't."

She smiled. "Heather," she said simply. "I like to listen to music."

"She sings too!" said Brother Paul. "Heather sang the national anthem at the high school football game last year."

"Yes, but actually, it was two years ago," she said quietly, seemingly a little embarrassed.

"Maybe you'll sing for us on the trek," said Brother Paul hopefully.

"I don't know," Heather replied. "I kind of have a cold."

"Oh, well, we've got two weeks. Maybe your cold will get better."

"Maybe," she answered. But Katie wasn't convinced. She was sure that getting that girl to sing for them would be like getting Katie's mother to stop drinking.

"And the last one of our family to arrive gets to go last. It's your turn!" Brother Paul said, turning his gaze upon Katie.

She had thought during all of the other introductions what she might say, but couldn't think of anything that would do. "Hi, my name's Katie, and I like to steal iPods from lockers." Or "I'm Katie McBride, and I like to hit my mom," each occurred to her. But those confessions might be a little shocking to this bunch.

"My name is Katie," she finally said. "And I like . . . I like . . ." Here Katie looked off into the distance and, tilting her head and shaking it back and forth slowly, at length said, "I have no clue" as if it were a revelation to herself. Then after a big sigh and as if she had just thought of it, Katie added, "I like hiding my mother's bottles of scotch under the porch, though. She hasn't found them there yet!" Or had she? The thought occurred to Katie suddenly. And then she blinked her eyes long and hard and opened them wide as she realized how stupidly she had just spoken. *Why, oh why, can't I learn to just keep my mouth shut?*

Each member of Katie's new family seemed to stare at her exactly as did Mrs. Maxwell when Katie had told her why she had gone to juvenile court. Their stares declared, "What you're saying is totally foreign to my little world. I don't have the slightest idea how to respond."

Noticing their discomfort, Katie added quickly, "I mean, who really has a clue about what they really like anyway? I don't even know why I said that."

This clarification, however, did very little to put the group at ease. Brother Paul cleared his throat again, though, and said with a smile not quite as brilliant as the one he had displayed heretofore, "Welcome to you, Katie. We're so glad to have you in our group. Now," he began, obviously relieved that that was over, "it's Ma's turn. Mary, why don't you introduce yourself?"

Sister Paul stood a little taller, all the barely five feet of her, and said, "Well, my name is Marianne Paul, and I am really excited to be your ma for the next two weeks. And . . . one of my favorite things to do is read. I can spend hours reading."

She reminded Katie of Mrs. Maxwell. Mrs. Maxwell was short too, and she had read every book that anyone in the class had ever mentioned to her. But wait . . . the low pitch of her voice, her height, and the deep brown color of her hair were just like . . . . No, it was. . . . It was for sure! Sister Paul was the woman in the bathroom who had spoken so terribly about Katie's mother that her mother never returned to church. There was no doubt in Katie's mind. Her new ma was the person who was responsible for destroying the only real hope Katie had seen in the last six years.

Nine

"Katie, darlin', wake up! Please, dear," pleaded Madeline. "Aye, and I fear, m'lady to tell you, but all black hell's broken loose now!"

"What? What is it?" asked Katherine with a croaking voice.

"Beelzebub hisself is after sendin' up fierce, monstrous, and mangy beasts from his kingdom below! Aye, I heard tale of dragons which breathe out fire to destroy the earth; but only with a single look at all from one of these beasts, Katie, and the dragon would be runnin' for its life!"

Having become accustomed to Maddie's exaggerations, Katherine took her time lacing her shoes, fastening her hair up in a knot, and tying on her bonnet. She then wondered about Isaac, though he often got up in the morning before his mother did. "But where is Isaac, Maddie? Is he out slaying your fierce beasts?" teased Katherine, though she was actually somewhat worried.

"Not to be alarmed, me dearie. Isaac be seated on the buckboard keepin' a vigilant eye."

Katherine pulled the curtain aside, and, climbing out onto the buckboard, she was amazed to see a dark, rolling, breathing sea of mammoth animals. "Bison," she involuntarily whispered.

"Yes, Mother," Isaac whispered in response. "Thousands of them."

Katherine saw Nathanial before he saw her. At the James's

wagon behind them, he was helping Brother James mount a newly repaired wheel to the back axle.

"That should do it!" she heard Nathanial say. "At least until the next big bump. Let me know when that happens. Maybe we'll try some wire next time." He smiled then and his smile and his kindness, though directed at Brother James, reached Katherine. Her own face lit with a smile.

Look at that smile! He loves helping people—he seems to live for it.

At that moment Nathanial looked up and met her pleased glance. Katherine felt herself blush and turned toward Isaac.

"What a morning!" Nathanial called as he led his horse to Katherine's wagon. "Isn't this somethin'? In all my travels back and forth along the trail, only one other time have I seen buffalo like this!"

The bison marched as if to the beat of a slow drum, down from the northern butte to drink the river water. Like a black cloud of locusts on a crop of corn, trails and trails of buffalo moved down into and pushed ever wider the huge bulk of bison that spread over the flat grasses and filled the river. One buffalo, for some reason splitting from the herd, veered from the established march and neared the wagon train and then began traveling parallel to it.

"Wouldn't you like him for a pet, Isaac?" suggested Nathanial. "I don't know where you'd keep him, though."

"Hey, buffalo!" Isaac called out, though not loudly and with more than a little trepidation.

Taking no notice of him, the buffalo neither swung its gigantic head to the left nor to the right. Katherine had seen a buffalo head mounted on a wall in the governor's state house in Vermont. If that buffalo had appeared out of time and incongruent with modern day, even prehistoric, far more did this live specimen appear so. It was almost more believable to imagine the bison being swallowed up in a chasm of the earth to be carried back safely to its own time and place, for it certainly did not seem part of this almost desolate prairie wherein the company had been lucky to catch sight of a prairie dog or an antelope. Even birds were scarce. How could so many thousands of these huge beasts find enough to eat here? What would they eat in the winter?

Isaac grew braver. "Hey, buffalo!" he shouted again, loudly this time. "Look over here!" Taking off his hat, the black felt hat he had found off to the side of the trail a few days before, Isaac waved it in large sweeps in the air as he yelled.

Still the single buffalo marched on, refusing to notice the little boy seated on the buckboard. It was as if the reality of the bison was removed from their own—as if the buffalo through his huge eye saw and walked through a separate dimension, one without beginning or end, untouched by man, as free and unmarred as at its first creation.

It occurred to Katherine that she and the person to whom she wrote her journal were somewhat like that buffalo and Isaac—brought together, but at the same time separated by space or time, whether real or imaginary. And then a second thought came. *Perhaps Nathanial and I are like that too.*

"If we could harness these animals, we'd be in good shape. They appear mountains stronger than the horses and oxen pulling our wagons. Don't you think, Nathanial?" she asked.

"They're strong all right. But buffalo seem to have a mind of their own, Kate. Even the Indians who have shared this land with them forever live separate from them. It must be for a reason."

Katherine noticed Sarah carefully climbing out of the back of the Brighton's wagon. The wagon rested adjacent to Katherine's. "Good morning, Sarah! Quite a sight, isn't it?" she exclaimed.

Sarah nodded in agreement as she held her hands to her stomach. "I've never seen anything like them in my life."

"Anything else new this morning, Sarah?" Katherine had seen many pregnant women, including herself, but she had never seen anyone with a belly so perfectly and tightly round as Sarah's.

"No, not really," answered Sarah, grimacing as the baby's foot or hand poked her from the inside. Since the baby sat high, she ran out of air quickly and had to take a quick breath after every phrase. "Just the same contractions I've been having all week. Nothing any stronger."

"It's still early, isn't it?" asked Nathanial.

"A few weeks early, yes. I wouldn't be surprised, though, with all of the bouncing the baby's been getting on this wagon if he didn't come far before the day he's due."

"He, you say? You think it's a boy, then?" Katherine asked.

"Just a feeling, Katherine. You never know, though, do you?"

"You could name him Jacob, your first born son in the wilderness," suggested Katherine, laughing.

"Jacob . . . Jacob. I like it. Samuel wants to call him Wheeler after his mother's maiden name. I might have to let him have his way; after all, I named our Ann. But—Wheeler! We might as well call him Buckboard or Axle!"

"Well, I'm sure you'll get used to it if that is what you name him," Nathanial said, chuckling. "Wheeler. It's not too bad, really," he added, scrunching one eye and half his smile in an attempt to get used to the name himself.

Sarah laughed. "If the name causes everyone who hears it to make that kind of a face, the poor boy will be doomed his whole life."

Deeming it best to change the subject, Nathanial said, "I found a midwife to help you deliver. Sadie Passions. She's with the wagon train camped a few miles ahead of us. She says if we send a rider to get her, she'll come help when we need her."

"Thank goodness he has found someone, Sarah," said Katherine. "I wouldn't know the first thing to do. I'd probably pass out."

"Not you, Katherine," said Sarah. "I know you too well. Weren't you the one who bound up little Nellie's twisted ankle?"

"Ah, yes. But there was no blood there. Not a drop. It's the blood that scares me."

"Let's hope Sadie gets here then." Sarah laughed.

Sarah looked out at the vast streams of buffalo. "I don't think these buffalo will let us move on any time soon. It would be a perfect opportunity for us to get some bread rising," she suggested.

"Wonderful idea," agreed Katherine. "We'll let Madeline knead. She makes kneading dough look as easy as spreading jam on toast."

"Well, I'll leave you two to the bakin' and check on the rest of the wagons." Lifting his hat in good-bye, Nathanial left with his horse at a slow trot.

What is it about him? Why can't I get rid of this feeling? It's that . . . I like him. Okay, I admit it. I like him very much. . . . But Michael . . . Michael is waiting.

"I like him, Katherine," Sarah commented as she mixed the ingredients. "Nathanial, I mean. He reminds me of Michael, actually. Except, well . . . I know they're about the same age, but for some reason Nathanial seems older—like he's lived through a great deal more in his life perhaps. He just seems unusually wise—kind of like Solomon!" Sarah laughed. "Has he told you yet how he feels about you?"

I loved you, Kate—and I still do. I need to know if you might ever love me.

"Katherine?"

"Oh, I'm sorry. I was just thinking. The truth is, Sarah, that Nathanial has been quite busy with the wagon train lately. Hardly have we spent a few minutes together in the last two weeks. But he knows I'm faithful to Michael. It would be unlikely that he would do such a thing."

"Well, and of course he won't, darlin'," said Maddie, appearing suddenly at the back of the wagon. Isaac followed a short way behind her. "Yer man has his pride, he does. He's not after layin' his wee heart before you so's that you can smash it to pieces now!"

"Madeline, I do believe you have ears at the back of your head!" exclaimed Katherine.

"Aye, Katie, dearest, I pride meself on me hearin.' It be one o' me best characteristics, so it is! But you, girl, you're not after listenin' at all, at all, are you now?"

Shaking her head in disapproval, Maddie rolled up her sleeves to begin kneading. "Well, and enough said. I'll be leavin' the romancin' to you, ladies. Just leave all the kneadin' to me. They didn't call me the Baker of Londonderry for no reason, now did they?" she declared.

Isaac, who had pinched off a large piece of dough and was about to plop it in his mouth, interrupted. "But, Maddie, didn't you tell me before that they called you the Londonderry Bird?"

"Which is it, Maddie?" asked Katherine with a wink at Sarah. "Were you the Londonderry Bird or the Londonderry Baker? And didn't you also say you were the champion buggy racer of Londonderry?"

"Well 'n all three o' them, me dearies. All three to be sure," answered Maddie calmly. She in turn pulled up the dough with her fingertips and smashed it forward rapidly with the palms of her hands. "Though I've left the racin' behind me now, so it is. Me bones be altogether too brittle now for racin', to be sure. So ye might now call me the Bakin' Londonderry Bird or the Baker of Londonderry Which Danced. There ye 'ave it," Maddie declared as she heaped the dough into Katherine's large black kettle.

Tying a cloth on the kettle to cover the dough, Katherine hung the pot on a nail placed and curved just for that purpose at the back of the wagon. There the dough would rise as they traveled and be ready to bake when they stopped to camp.

"This will be a nice surprise today for Samuel," commented Sarah. "There's nothing he likes more than fresh, hot bread."

"Nathanial loves fresh bread, too," said Katherine. "He can smell it a mile away up the trail and makes sure he gets here for one of the first hot slices. And did I ever tell you that Michael—" But Katherine, realizing she had thought of Nathanial first, didn't finish.

"What?" asked Sarah. "What about Michael?"

Katherine turned and pretended to straighten the cloth

over the dough so that Sarah would not see the confusion on her face.

"Never mind, Sarah," Katherine said finally. "I've forgotten now."

For days Chimney Rock had stood as the focal point of the way west, but now, as the trail of wagons finally wound toward its base, a large band of Indians rode toward them from around the huge landmark.

"There must be almost a hundred of them!" Nathanial called out to Sam Brighton.

"You know what the paint means, Nathanial—it means war!" Sam called back.

The Indians were magnificent, framed by the brilliance of the setting sun. Seated unusually straight, their heads and shoulders raised tall to the sky, their faces drawn with bright colors, the braves had lined their horses at the foot of the rock. Their formation remained still, solid, and defiant as they awaited the pioneers. One aged Indian sat on his horse apart from the rest. He wore a large, ornate headdress of tall feathers and held a black-arrowed spear in one hand and reins in the other. Obviously the chief of the Indians, his hair was long, down to the middle of his back, and shone extraordinarily, as if silver metal were woven through it.

Katherine had never seen horses like theirs. Their coats glistened with splashes of deep, earthy colors—sienna, charcoal, and rust—as if each horse had been freshly painted from the dirt and clay of the earth. They were beautiful and spirited. The horses, though ridden, still somehow gave the sense of being wild and free, equal with and as much a part of the vast wilderness as were the long buttes, the rivers and streams, the tall grasses, and even the setting sun itself.

For some reason, as she drove her wagon slowly toward them, Katherine was not afraid. In fact, she wished it were possible to freeze the moment so that she could paint the scene; Katherine carried her paints and drawing paper in the back of the wagon. She would have to memorize the sight to later record it.

From the front of the train of wagons, where the Atkinson group was positioned that day, a signal came back, a whistle call with hands shaped in a half sphere. As they pulled up, the wagons began forming a tight circle, three and four wagons deep.

Holding a stick tied with a white cloth and sustaining their hands in the air to show they were unarmed, Jeb Hutchings, the leader of the wagon train, together with William Jackman, the guide who had lived a short time with the Indians, walked slowly but purposefully from the wagons toward the line of warriors. Katherine watched the faces of the Indians. Not one face turned or showed a change of expression. The dark feathers tied in their wild hair fluttered in the breeze.

Dismounting from his horse, which differed from the others in that it was larger and a solid black, the Indian chief met Brothers Hutchings and Jackman. The three struggled to communicate. They gesticulated with almost every word while the regiment of Indians remained immobile and the pioneers looked on in anticipation from the wagon circle. The men and a few women held their guns as they stood by their wagons. The remainder of the women quieted their children inside the wagons as the children ventured to peer out on occasion and then quickly popped their heads back inside.

After what seemed a very long period of time, an agreement was reached. With both arms raised, the chief turned to his warriors and spoke just three words. The Indians dismounted. A message was sent back to Nathanial and all the company captains, each being in charge of ten wagons, that all ninety-eight Indians—Katherine had counted them—were to be their dinner guests. Each wagon was to prepare an extra plate. Understanding that the Indians had feared the men in the wagon trains had come to take their land, Nathanial and the other leaders believed the Indians would no longer be a threat now that they knew the wagon train was merely passing through.

Glad they had started bread that morning, Sarah and Katherine, with help from Maddie and Isaac, dug a hole in the ground to fit the pot of risen dough. Then, after Sarah made sure the lid was set tight, Katherine placed buffalo chips from their stockpile on the lid and lit the chips.

"Thank heavens the chips are dry enough to catch fire," commented Sarah.

"Yes, and let's not forget to thank Sister Hutchings for her brilliant invention. Her buffalo-chip oven bakes bread just as well as my new butterfly stove did in Nauvoo," added Katherine.

Over the fire, the women then fried a pound of dried bacon and boiled ears of corn, which they had purchased a few miles back, for the two families and their Indian guests. Then, when the bread was baked, Maddie cut off two thick slices for the plates of the Indians and spread the slices with the last of the butter, scraped from the bottom and sides of the butter crock.

"No matter," said Maddie. "I'll be visitin' me new friend Helen one of these next days, and to be sure she'll save a wee little cream for us from her sweet cow, and then we'll have us some more butter."

"Bread and butter, bacon and corn. Not a bad meal here in this wilderness," said Sarah.

"Aye, in faith, me ladies!" confirmed Maddie.

Food in the camps was usually simple, meager, and unvaried. When they camped near a river or stream, Nathanial and Isaac would often go fishing and bring back enough for a meal. The sugar and molasses had run out many miles earlier. Sarah and Katherine were allotted weekly, however, a fair amount of flour and bacon—though each week the amount given to them was less—and at times they found wild gooseberries to sprinkle on top of pancakes for breakfast. Just as Sarah and Katherine hung the pot of bread dough to rise at the back of the wagon, they could hang a wooden churn containing cream, and the bumpy ride would turn the cream to butter by the end of the day's travels.

On two previous occasions, a hunter in the wagon train had shot buffalo and divided the meat among the camps. With more than one hundred wagons in the train, though, the meat disappeared quickly. William Jackman, who had been Maddie's guide from Winter Quarters to the wagon train, had shown the company how to jerk buffalo meat over a small fire and cut the hides to make ropes, halters, and sandals. While it lasted, they used the bone marrow to cook with in the place of butter. Mr. Jackman had even taught the company how to use buffalo hair to stuff their bed mats and pillows.

Isaac asked a blessing on the food, and then Sam carried two tins of dinner to Jeb Hutchings' wagon, where the Indians were all gathered.

Later the men of the camp were called together. As women and children looked on from the dark, the men sat circled with all ninety-eight Indians around a huge, sweltering fire, each of their faces illuminated by the light of the blaze. The bright circles, lines, and zigzags of red, yellow, and black paint on the Indian faces were magnified in the dim light making them almost phosphorescent.

Katherine saw a very young Indian—perhaps no more than sixteen or seventeen years old—pass a peace pipe to Nathanial. She was too far away to see Nathanial's eyes, but the image of his eyelashes against his skin again sunk deep.

As the pipe circled from hand to hand and mouth to mouth, its swirling smoke became a weak sibling to the explosion of smoke from the campfire. No one spoke. It was as if they all, the seated pioneers and Indians and the women and children who looked on, were joined in some sort of trance, each pulled to the others by the rolling colors and heat of the flames. At that moment they were all the same: the lines of age around the mouths of the Indian and the white man as they pressed their lips around the pipe, the lines of laughter or concern around their eyes as they closed them tight to suck in deeply. The slight smiles. They were all the same, whether on Indian lips or white.

June 21

Dear Someone to Whom I Write,

The day has been good. Our Lord is full of tender mercies toward all of his children wherever they are, whether in cities or on the plains, in brick houses or in tepees. He knows and loves them all. The Spirit testifies to me that the natives of this land are loved by Him just as much as, and perhaps even more, than are we. They are like the land: beautiful, proud, and with a quiet wisdom that is perhaps from the earth itself. We walk along their corridor. This has been their trail west for many hundreds of years. As soon as we make a stop that is long enough, perhaps this next Sunday, I will try to paint them. And I'll leave the painting here in these pages for you so that you can see them just as I did.

Katherine

Ten

"What do you see on this paper? Do you see the tiny black dot in the center or do you see the white all around it?"

"I see slimy sweat trickles running down your face and gigantic wet, dark rings growing bigger by the minute under your armpits. That's what I see, so let's get on with this," said Katie. Fortunately she spoke quietly and stood apart from the congregation of trek-goers. Having all traveled for many hours by car or truck to an open dust field out in the middle of nowhere, which was to be the staging or take-off area, they now listened intently to a tall man in long shirt sleeves and a tie. His suit seemed rather out of place amid a swarm of cowboy hats and hiking boots. The crowd was quiet, if not silent, though, and noticeably expectant.

"You see," continued the man with a heavy, small-town-Utah accent, "you can find what's difficult about this trek—the small black dot. Or you can find the whole lot of good—the white—that it's all about. You and your handcart family will be together for two weeks, rain or shine. No one needs a grump."

"This will be a trek that could change your life. Let me say as Lehi did to his sons when he knew he was nearing death, 'Awake my sons [and might I add daughters]; put on the armor of righteousness. Shake off the chains with which ye are bound, and come forth out of obscurity, and arise from the dust.'"[1]

He must be joking, thought Katie. *We're up to our ankles in dust already, and we're not even on the trail yet. There's no way anyone will be arising from the dust on this trek!*

Standing on a platform so that all could see and hear him, the man now straightened his stance, cleared his throat, and began reading from a book that appeared much like a Bible:

"'The Word and Will of the Lord concerning the Camp of Israel in their journeying to the West: Let all the people of the Church of Jesus Christ of Latter-day Saints, and those who journey with them, be organized into companies, with a covenant and promise to keep all the commandments and statutes of the Lord our God.'

"Why were the Saints organized into companies in 1847, and why are we now? Because they needed a group to belong to and to depend upon in order to make the journey. And so do each of you. That's why you're organized into families. Help your family out. Share the load and help with the load of anyone who needs a hand. That's what it's all about."

Clearing his throat once again, the man continued reading. "'And this shall be our covenant—that we will walk in all the ordinances of the Lord.'"[2]

The man then paused briefly and resumed speaking with a less elevated voice. "Now—don't walk too close to the wheels of the carts. We don't want anyone to get hurt. Also—if you need to . . ."

"And this shall be our covenant—that we will walk in all the ordinances of the Lord," repeated Katie in her mind. *You'd have to really trust in God to make a commitment like that. I can't even trust myself,* thought Katie.

"Keep a prayer in your heart the whole time," continued the man. "Pray that you'll see and feel what the pioneers who crossed the plains went through. Most of them who started in Iowa took about 121 days to make it. You're trekking fourteen days and at a much slower pace. It won't be easy for you, though. You already know it wasn't easy for them.

"Their testimonies of the true and living God drove them to do what they did. And they did not regret their sacrifice. One pioneer who suffered starvation, freezing snows, and deaths all around him, said this about his experience when, years later, the decision to allow the Willie Handcart Company to cross the plains was questioned:

"'You are discussing a matter you know nothing about. Cold historic facts mean nothing here for they give no proper interpretation of the questions involved. Mistake to send the handcart company out so late in the season? Yes. But I was in that company and my wife was in it and Sister Nellie Unthank whom you have cited was there, too. We suffered beyond anything you can imagine and many died of exposure and starvation, but did you ever hear a survivor of that company utter a word of criticism? . . .

"'I have pulled my handcart when I was so weak and weary from illness and lack of food that I could hardly put one foot ahead of the other. I have looked ahead and seen a patch of sand or a hill slope and I have said, I can go only that far and there I must give up, for I cannot pull the load through it.

"'I have gone on to that sand and when I reached it, the cart began pushing me. I have looked back many times to see who was pushing my cart, but my eyes saw no one. I knew then that the angels of God were there.

"'Was I sorry that I chose to come by handcart? No. Neither then nor any minute of my life since. The price we paid to become acquainted with God was a privilege to pay, and I am thankful that I was privileged to come in the Martin Handcart Company.'"[3]

Then lowering his book and the volume of his voice, the man with the tie stated, "I testify to you that God the Father lives. Jesus is the Christ. Joseph Smith was a prophet. Our ancestors came across the plains because they believed these things too."

Katie stood silent, her mind quiet and deep. How could he know those things? He sounded like he really knew. Unable or perhaps unwilling to shake the pervasive, calming peace with which his words blanketed her, Katie remained still. Even her right foot, which normally tapped or wiggled incessantly, kept quiet contact with the earth. It was a feeling unlike any she had felt before—an all-is-right-with-the-world peace, a don't-worry-I'll-take-care-of-you kind of comfort. Katie had never felt taken care of before.

Soon she felt a hand at her elbow. It was Brother Paul. "Let's head out!" he said to her with excitement. Already a moving line of handcarts and pioneers stretched out northward, blotches of laughter and color fading into the distance on the trail before them. Handcart twenty-two, Katie's handcart, was the last in the line. Cracked, splintered, and metal-rimmed, the two wooden wheels of the cart were huge, almost reaching Katie's shoulders. And now those wheels began rolling.

Katie's gaze followed the line of handcarts to its beginning and then searched onward to find a hint of their destination. There was no endpoint, however. A wide expanse of flat, dry land, stretched out before her, relieved only by occasional blotches of cloud shadows, crumbly hills of rock and sand, tufts of dying sagebrush, and of course, the "pioneers" and their handcarts.

The bed of cart twenty-two measured no more than six by five feet. Inside, sleeping bags, boxes of food, and eight plastic buckets, including Katie's, were jammed together and fighting for space. As the family of trekkers journeyed along the trail, a bag of rolls or some other essential item often found itself shoved off the side of the cart onto the trail behind them. Now it was Micah's sleeping bag that rolled in the dust.

Micah opened her mouth wide in disbelief. "Ugh!" she cried out. "And I'm supposed to sleep in that tonight?"

"Time for a readjustment!" Brother Paul called out. "Let's get these puppies in tighter."

"Hey, Pa?" It was Morgan. "We might try tying the rope around the tarp on the inside instead of outside the cart. I don't know, but I think things will stay in better that way."

"Good man," replied Brother Paul. "Let's do it."

Lindsay and Zach helped Brother Paul and Morgan tuck the tarp and rope inside the edges of the cart bed. Wrapping the last length of rope over the top of the tarp-covered load, Brother Paul slip-knotted the rope and pulled hard until the rope was so tight it would be difficult to stick a knife under it. "I think that'll do it," said Brother Paul. "Great idea, Morgan. I like how you think."

Katie watched in amazement as Morgan once more positioned himself inside the tongue of the handcart and began pushing. This time Lindsay, who was definitely not the most physically fit of the little family, offered to push at his side.

Doesn't he ever quit? It's not like he's going to win a prize or anything.

The dust rose up from the cart in front of them, and Katie began feeling dirt inside her throat and nostrils. "We need handkerchiefs," said Sister Paul as she covered her mouth and nose with her bonnet. "The pioneers tied them around their faces to filter out some of the dust."

Wow, two weeks of this dust, thought Katie. *Our lungs will need pumping by the time we're through.*

Sister Paul—Ma—slowed so that Katie would catch up with her. "So," said Ma, "did your parents put you up to this trek or was it your own idea to come? I have to confess, I'm here because Daniel—your pa—is here."

Katie had not forgotten her discovery of who "Sister" Paul really was. "Well, Ma, you see I prayed about it, and a glorious angel with white feathery wings appeared to me and told me that I must go on this trek today. My parents didn't believe me about the angel, but they let me come anyway."

Seemingly unruffled, Ma responded, "I saw an angel once myself, but my angel didn't have wings."

Katie was curious about Ma's angel, but she didn't want to give her the satisfaction of asking about it. "Then we've both seen one. I guess we have one thing in common," replied Katie, emphasizing the "one" in "one thing."

"You look familiar to me for some reason," said Ma. "Have we met before?"

"Not unless it was in a dream," replied Katie as they trudged along side by side. "Maybe you saw me in a choir of angels that sang behind the angel you saw." Katie didn't want to tell her they had met in the church bathroom. Not yet, at least.

"Maybe," said Ma with a slight laugh. "If so," she added after a pause, "you must have been the brightest and most beautiful angel singing at the top of the choir."

Katie's step slowed. Could Ma really have said what Katie thought she had heard? Katie would have in fact stopped completely if the turning wheels of the handcart hadn't already become a fixed part of her own motion. Why would Ma say that? She had never considered herself bright nor beautiful.

"Water break!" called out Pa. It seemed that they hadn't traveled for very long, but the elevation of the sun in the sky proved differently. Katie filled her tin cup with cold water from the five-gallon jug at the bottom corner of the cart. Though jammed tightly against the corner, it bounced together with the other supplies and continually leaked or splashed water on the contents of the cart that surrounded it. The jug left a trail of water in the dust as the cart rolled along.

The water was cool against Katie's sun-baked, dusty lips and somehow tasted sweeter and more delicious than any water she had tasted before. She sat alone on a rock a short distance from the trail to rest and drink. There was something about this trek and these people. Something different. They were good people—well, most of them at least. And they believed in something that made them good—and seemed to make them happy. *Maybe*, thought Katie as she turned her chin to the sun, *maybe goodness brings happiness*. She thought about that for a minute and then shook her head. No, that was them, not her. She wasn't born to be good. She couldn't be. It wasn't in her blood.

Out of the corner of her eye, Katie noticed a tiny bird near her, just standing there on a rock, probably a sparrow. Turning her head slowly toward the bird so as not to scare it, Katie stretched her finger out toward it.

"Hi, little bird," Katie greeted with her softest and quietest voice. The bird turned its head sharply toward her, as if its head swung on a hinge. Its eyes, like tiny ornamental, plastic beads, fixed themselves on Katie.

"You're like me, aren't you, girl? Off by yourself."

Proving her wrong, the bird abruptly flew up and landed in a nearby scrub oak tree amongst many other similar birds. They all started chattering at once. It appeared that the tree itself suddenly began blurting out its own nonsensical chitchat.

"Hey, Katie!" It was Micah walking toward her. Katie was surprised that Micah didn't have her pom-poms with her. She might as well have brought them; she was consistently set in cheerleader mode. "I saw your birdie friend fly off."

Katie didn't know what she was supposed to reply to that, so she said nothing.

Micah, obviously offended by Katie's silence, folded her arms high under her chest and narrowed her already squinty eyes. "I guess you think you're too good to talk to me." Still Katie did not respond.

Micah took a deep breath and continued. "Well, I know better. The kids at school tell me you're a loner—a thief. That you're always in trouble. So if you don't want to talk to me, that's okay. At least I tried." And with that Micah unfolded her arms, turned sharply, and marched off, her yellow bonnet swinging at her back behind her.

Many in the little group seemed eager to be off after their short break. As soon as they had taken position at the tongue of the cart, Zach and Morgan began running, in fact, to gain momentum up a small hill in front of them. The old cart bounced and veered horribly behind them, looking as if it might capsize at any second. When Ma commented that the boys looked like clowns in a circus act, Katie couldn't help herself—she laughed together with Ma. And then Pa turned around and winked at Katie. *Is it just a big front? Do they really like me or is it all pretend?*

Going down the hill wasn't as easy as going up, though. Katie helped Pa and Lindsay hold back the momentum of the cart as Morgan and Zach walked it slowly down the hill. Even with the three of them holding the cart back, they had to dig their boots deep into the loose dirt and pull hard at the hand-cart to prevent it from running into the backs of the two boys.

"Next time," said Pa as they made it to the bottom, "we'll turn the cart around. I'll bet we can control it better if we back it down the hills."

"Good idea," agreed Morgan. "I like how you think, Pa."

Chuckling to himself, Pa slapped Morgan on the back and said, "Okay! Let's be off! We're burnin' daylight. Who's gonna pull?"

"I'll try," offered Katie, surprising even herself.

"And I'll pull with you," said Heather.

It wasn't as hard to push at the tongue of the handcart and make it roll as Katie thought it would be. Perhaps it was because there were two pulling together and because the way was now flat.

"I've seen you around school," commented Heather, obviously searching for something to say.

"I've seen you too," replied Katie.

"Don't you hang with Gustavo Palacio and Stephen Fry?"

"Sometimes, I guess," was Katie's reply. "When they come to school."

"I've never seen you at church, though," said Heather.

Surprised at Heather's statement, Katie momentarily stopped pushing. "That's 'cause I don't go, obviously," she finally answered.

Heather quickly looked away from Katie. "Well, I mean, I've seen your name on class rolls sometimes at church."

Softening the tone of her voice, Katie explained. "I guess that's because my mother is actually a member of your church. Not me, though. I've only been there twice in my life. Does Sister Paul—Ma—does she go to church where you do?" asked Katie.

"Sure, the Pauls are in my ward, the Longview 2nd Ward. That's why they already knew me. Why?"

"And is your church the one where we all met this morning?" persisted Katie.

"Yes, that's it. Why?" asked Heather one more time, catching breaths now between her words as they began to climb.

"Nothing. I just thought I remembered her from once when I was there."

Katie and Heather were then quiet as they concentrated all their energy on lugging the six to seven hundred pounds of handcart and supplies up the small hill. As the way became steeper, the cart slowed until it only crawled. Beads of sweat formed on Katie's face, and Heather's light blue blouse splotched dark and wet. The joints of the handcart squeaked and moaned.

Just when Katie thought she could push no further, however, the handcart suddenly became light and seemed to be pushing itself up the hill. Turning around, Katie and Heather smiled to see Morgan and Zach pushing the handcart from behind. "Just a little help for our friends," panted Morgan. And soon they were at the top.

Late that afternoon when handcart twenty-two finally rolled down into a meadow that lay at the base of several low hills where the company would camp for the night, Morgan and Pa led the cart. The three deep-green, portable outhouses which seemed to magically appear around the bend after every two hours or so, welcomed them into their home for the night. A half dozen or more campfires greeted them as well, started by other handcart families and now burning brightly throughout the meadow. A group of ten or twelve people stood in a huge circle as they threw and caught bright-colored Frisbees; others at one far end seemed to have just begun a sack race, while many more stood or sat around campfires, eating out of tin pie plates. Katie sighed happily at the end of their march. Rest. And dinner. A smoky, barbeque-ish aroma hung over the meadow.

"That will be beans and bacon—our meal for tonight!" Ma announced.

The family situated themselves in a vacant area of the camp, and Katie watched Pa start a fire and Ma open a gigantic can of pork and beans and pour it into a cast-iron skillet. The other skillet was filled with bacon pieces, and soon the bacon began sizzling. Untying her bonnet, Katie took it from around her neck and set it on the grass. She slid her fingers along the neckline of her dress to free her skin from the heat, but her fingertips grated against dirt. Katie felt the back of her neck. It too was covered with grime. Even her eyebrows were dusty. Using her bonnet, Katie wiped the dirt from her as best she could. This bonnet is good for something, I guess. She wondered how long it would be until they would come to a river where they could wash.

"Hey, Katie, will you give me a hand over here?" It was Morgan. "Just hold this pole while I set up the other pole, and we'll have you a tent." Unable to think of a good reason not to help, and since it was to be the girls' tent, after all, Katie walked over.

"Look that way," said Morgan as Katie held the pole, and he secured the tent. His look pointed in the direction of the setting sun. Katie could see many light, circular patches of ground in areas of less brush. A sticklike object stood at the center of many of the circular areas.

"What are they?" asked Katie.

"Prairie dogs. They stand board-stiff halfway in and halfway out of their holes."

Katie stared fixedly at one backlit by the setting sun just up the hill. Sure enough, she could see that it was an animal. A tawny light-yellow color, the prairie dog stood so still it looked preserved and stuffed. As Katie and Morgan watched, it stood against the skyline without moving, statuelike, seemingly forever. It appeared to be looking out for danger.

"Watch what happens," said Morgan. "Follow me."

Morgan began quietly climbing the hill with Katie stepping lightly behind him. As they came closer, Katie heard clucking and chirping noises, and the prairie dogs began slipping back into their holes. They popped down left and right, some even down into holes in the trail they had earlier traversed to arrive at the meadow.

"I think they make that noise to warn the others," explained Morgan.

"I guess they think we'll hurt them," said Katie. "They drop down by instinct."

"Kind of like you," said Morgan unexpectedly, looking her directly in the face. "I've been watching you today. Anytime anyone gets at all close to you, you drop back down into your hole," finished Morgan.

He waited for a reply, but Katie only turned her gaze to the one prairie dog left standing.

"I think you're scared, just like the prairie dog, scared that people will get too close to you."

Katie remained quiet.

"The problem is," continued Morgan, "that you'd see a whole lot more if you kept your head up. There's a lot of world out there to see."

"Maybe. And maybe not. Maybe there's nothing worth seeing," Katie finally said as the last prairie dog popped down out of the reflection of the sun.

"Thanks for setting up our tent," she added as she ran back down the hill.

What business is it of his if I pop my head up or down? thought Katie, once inside her tent with her sleeping bag and storage bucket. What does he know? His dad didn't leave him—he goes hiking with his dad! And I bet his family isn't on welfare and that he doesn't have a mother who gets drunk every day.

After untying her sleeping bag and rolling it out flat, Katie sat on it without moving for a few seconds and then reached into the bottom of her bucket to lift out the diary. Opening it up gently, she noticed a name written on the inside cover of the journal that she had not noticed before. It was difficult to decipher, being written across an ornate blue pattern. Since it was becoming slightly dark inside the tent, Katie turned on her flashlight and directed it toward the name. *It can't be!* But it was. The name written in the journal was Katherine May McBride, Katie's own name!

Eleven

A never-ending sea of sagebrush sparsely carpeted the land before them, a sad substitute for the tall, green grasses of the meadow they had left behind shortly after dawn. The only reminders of modern civilization—gigantic, steel power-line towers—trudged into the huge valley from over the tops of the hills on the distant horizon, a chain gang of steel skeletons confined by stretches of electrical lines that bound each one to the next.

The heat was intense. Katie never ceased to be amazed at how quickly the desert morning chill evaporated into the stifling heat of the day.

"So when do we get baths?" asked Katie, walking behind the handcart. "Are the bathhouses just around the corner, or is there an Olympic-size pool built right over that hill for us to jump into?"

"'Fraid not," answered Pa. "But I'd be glad to hold the water jug over your head and give you a good splash. It's not the same as a swimming pool, but it's a close second."

"I'll go for that," said Morgan. Zach and Heather agreed.

"Ma?" called out Pa. "You and Lindsay hold up there. We're gonna have us a water break."

Standing on top of a large rock at the side of the trail, Pa held the water jug over Morgan's head. "Ready?" he asked.

"Ready," answered Morgan, positioning his head directly

under the spout. Water ran down his face and over a giant smile.

"This feels so good!" he exclaimed. Reaching up to the spout, he filled his palms with water and splashed Katie. "Come on in!" he said to her.

Katie wiped the water droplets from the side of her face. "Maybe I will," she said. The jug wasn't a swimming pool, but water was water, and she would take it any way she could get it.

Standing under the spout, Katie closed her eyes and waited. Pa pushed the button and cool, clear water immediately began to wash the heat away. With the water running over her closed eyelids, over and inside her open mouth, and then drenching her shoulders, Katie felt almost clean again.

A memory flashed in Katie's mind, something she had forgotten. She and her mother were at a park, sitting on a picnic blanket. Katie was about six or seven years old, and they were at a birthday party for one of Katie's good friends. Clouds began to load the sky; a few scattered, heavy raindrops fell; and then there was a crack of thunder.

"If we hurry, we'll beat the rainstorm!" someone said.

Katie remembered the frantic clean-up: mothers and daughters piling up party plates of half-eaten slices of cake, dumping out cups of lemonade in the grass, and gathering balloons and crepe-paper ribbon—all the color stashed quickly in the trash can. Katie recalled the hasty good-byes, some simultaneous, some called from close by, some from a far distance.

Snatching her purse and Katie's party favors from under a tree where she had set them, Katie's mother grabbed Katie's hand, and they began to run. The downpour caught them, however, just as they were about halfway to the car. Katie's mother laughed and stopped to look at Katie, and they laughed together at the rain that drenched their hair and dripped off their noses. The day was warm, and the rain felt wonderful.

"We may never get another chance to sing together in the rain, Katie," pronounced Katie's mother, and at a skip, still holding Katie's hand, she took off singing, just like she was in a Broadway musical.

"We're singin' in the rain. Just singin' in the rain! What a glorious feelin'. I'm happy again!"

Katie skipped and sang along with her mother.

She was right, thought Katie. *We never did get another chance. Everything changed.*

Micah's voice jolted Katie back to the present. "Just don't get the water on my face," Micah instructed as she tilted her head so that the water would run down her back.

Every morning thus far in the girls' tent, Micah had applied her makeup very carefully. How Micah passed her makeup and mirror through the bucket check, Katie would probably never know, but she guessed Micah had carried them hidden on herself somehow. Perhaps she had a secret compartment strapped to her leg under her dress. Or maybe she had a big pocket sewn into her bloomers. Whatever the case, Katie couldn't imagine who Micah was trying to impress. Zach, who didn't even seem to know what a girl was? Pa? Couldn't be. Maybe Morgan. Katie had to admit that Morgan wasn't bad looking. Perhaps, though, Micah was just one of those girls who never let anyone see them without makeup on.

Pa was last. "Good thing the water wagon is just ahead of us," said Pa as he shook to splash the water more evenly over himself. "Don't pour it all on me, though. We might get thirsty before we reach the wagon."

As Katie walked on at Morgan's side, her stomach gnawed and gurgled. The pioneer ash cakes they had all cooked for breakfast just didn't seem to fill the void, partly because Katie couldn't seem to get used to the idea of eating ashes. When they had first made them a few days ago, they had wet corn husks to wrap the batter in. Now, though, there were no more corn husks, so they just scraped flat rocks from around the fire until the rocks were as clean as possible and then patted a handful of the batter mix down on the rock. As soon as the top formed a crust, Pa told them to shovel embers and ashes from the fire on top of the corn mixture. When the ash cakes were done—about fifteen minutes later—they would brush the ashes off and break off any cindery parts. Katie could only pick at the center of her cake and throw the rest back into the fire. *No wonder so many of the pioneers died on the trail*, thought Katie. *Ash cakes are killers.*

Lunch didn't fill Katie either. Always eaten on the go, today's lunch was much the same as every day: dried fruit and biscuits. Sometimes they also had nuts or jerky. Once Ma opened the biggest can of peaches Katie had ever seen. It was gone in less than three minutes.

Though Katie had often gone hungry at home when her mother had drunk up all their food money, this was different. With all of the walking Katie was doing—and much of it at an incline—the energy income on the trek didn't seem to be nearly as much as the energy expenditure. Her stomach growled again.

"Is that your stomach or mine that keeps roaring?" asked Morgan.

"Mine. I'm so hungry. I feel like my legs need some food to keep them going. Is your stomach growling too?"

"Always," replied Zach. "I'm sure dinner is still a ways away. Maybe I can rustle us up a snack."

Quickening his step to catch up with Ma, Morgan quietly spoke to her. Ma turned to look back at Katie and then said something to Morgan.

"I told her you were extremely hungry," said Morgan as he met back with Katie. "You do feel like fainting, don't you? I told her you did. You said you didn't know if your legs could keep going."

"Fainting! I can't believe you said that. And I thought both of us were hungry, not just me!"

"Oh, well. It was just a tiny—the very tiniest—white lie," Morgan justified, demonstrating the size of the lie with his thumb and index finger. The lie looked to be no more than an eighth of an inch thick.

"And here it comes." Morgan smiled as Ma walked back to them, carrying something that definitely looked like food in her hand.

"Beef jerky! Thanks, Ma," said Morgan as he gave Ma a big side hug.

"Shh!" Ma cautioned. "I don't know if I can supply everyone with this. We might run short of food at the end. Anyway, this is for Katie, not you."

"Thanks, Mrs. Paul—I mean, Ma," said Katie, almost politely. Immediately she bit into a piece of the jerky Ma handed to her in a bag. It was the tastiest and most welcome beef jerky Katie had ever eaten.

Morgan didn't dare to have any while Ma walked with them. As soon as Pa called her away, however, he quickly took a piece and, in fact, devoured two or three pieces within the next five minutes.

"It's convenient to have a fainting damsel by your side," said Morgan.

"Very convenient," agreed Katie with a laugh.

"I didn't really do it for me, though. Really. I think you need someone to watch out for you. So I elected me."

Katie averted her eyes to the hillside and wondered how she could possibly respond to that. Morgan's remark amazed her. *Why would anyone want to care for me?*

Fortunately, Pa diverted Morgan's attention. "It's the Green River!" Pa called out. "I didn't think we were this close. There's your swimming pool, Katie!"

Sure enough, as they rounded the valley, a bend of the river sparkled in the sun.

"That's what all those 'yahoo's' have been about that we've been hearing from the handcarts up ahead," said Ma.

As they came nearer the river, Katie could see that it was much bigger than she thought it was at first glimpse. It stretched perhaps more than two hundred feet wide. Grassy banks alternated from one side to the other, and huge poplar trees threw varying bits and strengths of shade across the water.

"How old do you think those trees are, Ma?" asked Zach.

"Oh, I don't know. They look quite old. But I really don't have any idea," she replied.

"I wonder if they're the same trees that were here when the pioneers crossed," Zach said.

"I don't know. But if not these, I'm sure the ancestors of these trees were here." Indeed, except for a few power poles and lines in the distance, and a few fences here and there, the scene seemed much as it must have been when the pioneers camped by the river.

"It looks harmless now," said Pa, "but these rivers often ran fast and deep. Crossing rivers was usually the most dangerous activity the pioneers faced. They'd been on the trail several months before they reached a river, and they were exhausted and stretched to their limits. Imagine how difficult it would be to cross a flooding river with a train of wagons or even with handcarts piled high with goods. Many of the pioneers drowned."

In the quiet that followed Pa's words, and as if to echo him, three killdeer took flight from the bank of the river and flew out across the water, calling as they floated away. Though beautiful, their call was also haunting.

"Why did they do it?" asked Katie simply. "Why did they come? They could have just stayed in the East and been safe and sound."

"Actually that's not true," Pa answered. "It wasn't safe to live their religion anymore in Nauvoo. And they had been driven out of other areas as well. They needed a place where they could worship as they believed without threats and harm from others."

"But so many of them died," said Katie.

"It was a price they were willing to pay. They believed they were called to build the kingdom of God here on earth."

"I've read," added Ma as she looked out over the peaceful waters, "that many of the Latter-day Saints at that time believed they were actually the modern-day Israel. They believed themselves to be the newly chosen people of God and that their destiny was to fulfill prophecy and prepare the way for Christ's millennial reign."

Katie was quiet for a few moments as she gazed at a lone

gray bird perched atop a post marker that read, "California Trail."

"I don't know if I could pay that kind of price," she said finally, "even if I did believe all of that—even if I really believed God was real."

"Look!" said Morgan as he pointed upstream a few hundred yards. Two beautiful, large white pelicans with long orange beaks glided seemingly without effort across the water. The visible area of their great bodies remained motionless, the pelicans' legs performing the unseen work under the water.

The beliefs that drive people are sometimes so deep and so a part of them, Katie thought. *Like my ancestor who wrote the diary. Their heroism is what we see, though, not their beliefs. But without their convictions, they wouldn't be heroes. You have to believe in something to be a hero.*

The wheels of the handcart once again squealed loudly as Pa and Ma pushed the cart on and the others followed along, stepping through the grasses and dry tinder. Startled by the sudden noise, the two pelicans began flapping their huge white wings, which spanned perhaps six feet on each bird. It took some time for them to lift off, but when they did, the pelicans soared powerfully and splendidly together, bearing north over the river until they could be seen no more.

Moving on, Katie and her family soon heard plunging and splashing, shouts and laughter in the distance. Picking up speed, they quickly came upon the rest of the cart families spread along both banks of the river and sprinkled through a long stretch of the water.

"We'll cross here," said Pa. "But first—first, mind you— we'll swim awhile," he added with his usual big grin.

"But we don't have anything to swim in," complained Micah. "Why didn't they tell us to bring a swimming suit?"

Katie smirked. "I'll bet you're just dying to show off your new electric-orange tankini," she couldn't help saying.

"It's not orange," Micah responded quickly. "It's cocoa. At least that's what it said on the tag. We bought it on our last trip to New York, at Saks Fifth Avenue." Micah must have noticed Katie rolling her eyes, but she continued on in spite of—or perhaps because of—the disgusted look on Katie's face. "You have to go up to the tenth floor. Well, actually the elevator only goes up nine floors. You have to walk from there up to a small higher level. That's where the swimming suits are. Just in case you're ever in Saks Fifth Avenue. If you ever go to New York." She shot a sick, sweet smile back a Katie, a smile loaded with a strong dose of I'm-better-than-you.

Pa cleared his throat and spoke somewhat louder and at a higher pitch than usual. "Micah, you don't realize it, but this here is an opportunity. You swim around enough in your pioneer dress, and you'll wash it plum clean."

Pa turned his glance to the dirty—and most likely smelly—clothes of the rest of the family, and his voice regained its normal pitch. "We all need to swim around a lot," he advised.

"The pioneers camped and rested on Sundays, and that's when they washed their clothes too. Our schedule is the same. So we have to wait until Sunday to change and wash. We have a strong bar of soap and a washboard. That'll be fun," he added with a slight chuckle.

"Well, look what the trail dragged in," said the loud voice of a redheaded kid trudging out of the water to the bank. "It's cart number twenty-two!" he yelled to a bunch behind him.

"Let's get 'em!" called out a particularly scrawny boy. He looked determined, though—a fierce little ninja—and his legs almost flew out of the water as he headed toward them. What was worse, six or seven more teenagers and one huge adult followed close behind him.

It was like a scene out of *The Lord of the Flies.* Mrs. Maxwell had read it to the class. The boys looked crazed and wild, and they were taking the law into their own hands. It seemed there was no one to stop them: obviously realizing that the boys from cart twenty-one were only after the girls, the boys of cart twenty-two ignored the threat.

Maneuvering around the mob, Katie ran into the river and

dove under. If she was to get wet, she would do it herself. No one was going to throw her in. Ma did the same.

The redheaded boy and the adult ran toward Lindsay and Heather; the man easily picked Heather up, threw her over his shoulder, and headed toward the river. She came up coughing and spitting out water. Katie hoped there were no vocal-chord-attacking microorganisms in the river or Heather might never sing again.

Struggling to lift Lindsay, the redhead called for reinforcements.

"A little help, Dave!"

A big kid still in the water hurried to his aid.

All of the attackers then charged after Micah, who had run back down the trail to escape them. "No, not me!" she squealed. "I'm serious! Leave me alone!" She kicked as if she were being accosted in the slums of Detroit and screamed so loud that Katie was sure she could be heard at least a mile down the river. They threw her in anyway. Micah was soon as soaking wet as everyone else. Her face, though, differed from the rest of theirs: It dripped non-waterproof mascara.

"We'll get 'em back," said Morgan, who, along with the other guys, had waded into the river. "Climb up on my shoulders," he called to Katie. "We'll beat them all at chicken!"

Katie looked at Morgan and then at the boys from cart twenty-one, who were already stacking up to fight. She wasn't like them. Playing water chicken seemed kind of stupid, an easy way to make a fool of yourself.

First Ma climbed on top of Pa's shoulders; then Heather paired with Zach. Micah, surmising that Morgan was already taken, teamed up with Lindsay.

"We don't have a chance without you, Katie. C'mon—it'll be fun! Trust me," said Morgan.

Where have I heard that before? Oh, yeah. Gustavo. Trust me—meth is fun. Without having to think about it, Katie knew that the risk involved with trusting Morgan was zero compared to the risk of trusting Gustavo.

"Well, okay," agreed Katie.

Lowering himself into the water to provide easier access, Morgan grabbed on to Katie's ankles as she sat on his shoulders. She felt safe there. The feeling was instantaneous, and Katie wondered how she could just know that with Morgan she was safe.

They took off quickly. "All you have to do is drag them into the water," Morgan instructed Katie as they charged the team Morgan hoped to be the weakest pair—the ninja boy sitting on top of the redhead. "We win when you're the only one left sitting."

Stronger than he looked, the ninja fought with extraordinary tenacity. And the redheaded boy held on to him so tightly that it seemed impossible to knock him off. Someone, though—could it have been Morgan?—splashed water in the redhead's eyes, and when he let go of one ankle to rub his eye, Katie dethroned the ninja.

Actually, the other chickens were much easier to topple—even the big man, Brother Stevens, and his partner, a woman who was probably his wife. When Katie looked around for her next match, there was no one left.

Morgan danced around with Katie on his shoulders. "Who's bad, who's bad? Yeah, yeah! Who's bad, who's bad?"

"Okay," said Katie, noticing that everyone was looking at them. "We'll lose points for celebration. Let me down, all right?"

It was easy for Katie to play the other games now that she had begun: Marco Polo, King of the River Bend, games Katie had never heard of. She had to admit to herself that it was fun. And this place was Disneyland compared to Gustavo's little get-together and the nightmare that followed.

As she and Zach pulled the cart across the river to continue on the trek, though, Katie's feet dragged, even though Pa and Morgan pushed from behind. She couldn't remember ever feeling so worn out. In fact, having left most of their strength in the river, the entire company now inched slowly along the trail with the river behind them. To Katie, the cart seemed to have fattened up while it awaited them in the long grasses on the river bank.

"This cart needs to go on a diet," Katie said to no one in particular. "It feels like it gained two hundred pounds. Maybe we should throw some things out." She thought to ask the others if Lindsay was hiding in the cart under the tarp, but something unexpected happened. It occurred to Katie that the comment might make Lindsay feel bad, so she didn't say it. Surprised at herself, Katie raised her eyebrow, let out a little grunt, and pushed harder.

Zach and Katie soon stopped in their tracks, however, when they saw what awaited them. Two families before them struggled to push and pull their carts up an extremely steep and rocky hill. The wheels of their carts slipped back a foot or two each time ground was gained. It looked dangerous.

"Well, we won't climb it by standing here," Zach stated as he pushed his glasses back up across the bridge of his nose. "We can do it, Katie. Everyone will help."

"Go ahead and start up," said Pa. "As soon as you two get tired, some of us will take your places."

Katie looked down at the small rocks at her feet and then up at the progressively bigger rocks that led to the base of the hill and thought, *I'm already tired.* The river games had made her muscles feel like rubber bands. Nevertheless, for some reason, Katie couldn't manage to say no to Pa.

"Okay, let's go," she said to Zach.

As soon as they started up the bottom of the hill, it began to incline sharply. The rocks they stepped on and rolled over were squarish and cut sharply. It was difficult for Katie and Zach to keep their feet steady, let alone the wheels of the cart. Shimmying dramatically and creaking loudly at every drop, the wheels threatened at any moment to give up the ghost. Even with the rest of the family pushing from behind, Katie and Zach made headway very slowly. At this rate, it would take them an hour or two to top the hill.

About halfway up, a small jut in the hillside halted their progress completely.

"Let's all push together on three," Zach yelled to the family. "I think we can get it over!"

Katie wondered how any of them could put much force into the push. It took almost all of Katie's strength just to prevent the cart from slipping backward.

"Three!" called out Zach.

Katie gritted her teeth and shoved. The streams of sweat running down Zach's face splattered on her as his head heaved forward with the effort. Katie didn't flinch.

The two front wheels of the cart were rolling up and almost over the ridge when Pa fell. The loss of his weight against the cart had a huge impact. As it lurched backward, Katie's hands were suddenly forced tight against her stomach by the tongue of the cart. She found it difficult to breathe and felt as if the entire weight of the cart was against her. At her side, though, Zach was holding equal weight, and the others were all pushing from behind.

Pa rose quickly and added his weight against the cart, but it was too late. The cart had lost forward momentum and had begun slowly rolling backward.

Even if she tried, Katie did not think she could escape from the cart without injury to herself. And what about the others? She couldn't let them be crushed by the cart. Imagining one of the five-foot-tall wheels carrying the weight of the cart over Morgan or Lindsay or Ma, Katie looked to heaven and pled.

The bar crushed even more tightly against Katie's chest in response. Lindsay screamed as a huge splinter from the side of the cart pierced her hand. And then Lindsay let go. Someone wailed as the cart lurched back with greater momentum.

Then, as if by magic, new hands took hold and other shoulders heaved. New voices called out instructions. Brother Stevens and the five boys who had thrown the girls into the river appeared all around the cart, shoving and pulling. The cart stopped.

"We thought you were all gonners," confessed the ninja. "We didn't think we could make it in time. Good thing we did!"

"Good thing," said Pa. "A real good thing."

After shoving large rocks under the wheels to secure them tightly—they were taking no chances—everyone sat down to rest. Ma removed the splinter from Lindsay's hand, and after a while Brother Stevens and Pa took position at the tongue of the cart, while the five boys, along with Zach and Morgan, began pushing from the back and sides. Now there was little slippage; the wheels of the cart climbed the hill mechanically and force-fully, with little sway, as if commanded to do so.

Katie didn't even want to imagine what might have happened had help not arrived.

That night, movement in the camp was quiet and minimal. Around the campfire, the trekkers talked in low tones; the day had drained them all. From somewhere in a far corner of the camp, the soft, slow strumming of a guitar threaded through the sounds of the campfires: the hushed fall of wood; the infrequent, sharp snaps of sparks; the roar of the flames when fed with new fuel; and the swoosh of a marshmallow that had caught fire.

Katie sat on her bucket by the campfire that she had helped Zach and Morgan build. In her lap was her ancestor's journal. Katie knew it had to have been written by one of her ancestors. The author had the same name as hers, and the journal had been hidden in her house, which had belonged in the McBride family for generations. With only a little difficulty, she could make out the words by the light of the campfire, though the ink on the page was smudged as though by drops of rain.

June 30

Dear Friend,

I have not been able to write for some time. Isaac contracted cholera almost a week ago now. Many, a very many, have died of cholera on the trail. Will the Lord choose to take Isaac as he took Michael?

And then the letters of the writing suddenly became larger and darker, as if Katherine had interrupted her writing and then returned.

> *Without hope, though, there can be no faith. And without faith, there is little chance of a miracle. I will believe without doubt; I will rid my mind of any fear that enters. I will believe in the perfect love of a perfect Savior who gave His life and His very blood because of His love for me.*
>
> *The Lord will not take Isaac. The Spirit testifies now of that certainty in my heart. Oh, thank you, my Lord, my God. I will hope and I will be believing.*
>
> *Katherine*

Wow. This entry seemed more like a soliloquy than a writing to a friend as the other entries had been. Soliloquy. It was a term that Katie had learned in Mrs. Maxwell's class. To be or not to be—it was all about Hamlet figuring out for himself what he believed. *Hamlet* was the play they had studied in class at the beginning of the year. This was just like that.

Wow. This woman—with the same name as mine—was so good and had so much faith. She was like a rock: whatever happened to her, slammed or stormed around her, Katherine stayed true to her faith and to what she believed was right.

And she was my ancestor. We weren't all bad! Maybe there is some good, something solid and brave like her, in me. Maybe it has been there all along, but I just haven't looked hard enough to find it. Just maybe.

Twelve

With each step Isaac took, a new layer of mud encased the previous layer on his shoes until his feet were no longer feet at all but miniature mountains of mud, squishing in and sucking out of the westward trail. Rain drizzled on and on. Katherine had, in fact, lost track of when it had begun to rain. Four days ago? Five? Almost nothing was dry: dripping through the wagon cover, the rain soaked the bedding and yesterday's clothing, which had been stretched out to dry. The previous night, Maddie and Katherine considered themselves lucky that Nathanial was able to find them a large cottonwood tree under which to place the wagon for the night. But rain dripping from the leaves of the tree seeped through the canvas more readily than had the slow drizzle of rain in the open air.

"Mama, I don't feel well. I'm tired. And my stomach is making me hot."

Pulling back on the reins, Katherine stopped the animals. "Come up in the wagon then, Isaac, and trade me places. Maddie can drive the horses."

Isaac grabbed onto the buckboard and tried to lift himself up. "I can't, Mama," he said, dropping back to the ground. "I'm just too tired."

Climbing out of the wagon, Katherine lifted Isaac up to Maddie's arms. "Sure, he's burnin' with the fever," said Maddie, alarmed.

"Can I just lie down in the back for a while?" asked Isaac.

"O' course you can, me boy," replied Maddie as she helped him climb over the buckboard into the bed of the wagon.

Hurrying to the back to meet Isaac there, Katherine opened and reached into her trunk to pull out the only dry blanket remaining—the crocheted coverlet Michael had given her as a wedding gift. She placed her hand on Isaac's forehead.

"I've never felt a fever this high," she whispered to Maddie, as her eyes immediately filled with tears. There were nine she knew of who had died of cholera this last week. It began with weakness and fever.

Oh, Lord. Please, Lord. Not my son too.

"Let's get out of these wet clothes, Isaac," she said to him, unable to hide the emotion from her voice.

"Don't worry, Mama. I won't die like the others. I promise. You need me to help you. I won't let me die."

"I know you won't, Isaac." And then Katherine sobbed and had to wait before she continued. She wrapped the coverlet around Isaac's body. "I know you'll get well," she finally added. "You know I really need you. And you know I love you as much as there are stars in the heavens."

"From here to the Milky Way and back," said Isaac with his eyes closed.

"As big as the sun," added Katherine as she wiped the tears from her face. "You rest now. The best thing you can do is sleep." Katherine paused to control herself. "Maddie, will you send for Nathanial?"

"We've got to dry up the fever," pronounced old Jim Morely after he had examined Isaac. "Absolutely no liquids till the fever is gone. And have him wear these," he continued, holding out a long-sleeved flannel shirt and wool pants. "I took the liberty of finding some warm, dry clothing to bring to you. The clothing will help the fever to break."

"But, Jim, we're still in the middle of summer, and Isaac is already so hot he could almost light a fire!" objected Nathanial.

"I'm not a doctor, Brother Atkinson. But my father was. And this is always what he advised for fever. If you want the boy to get better, you'll do what I recommend."

"Thank you, Brother Morely. Thank you for coming and for the clothing. Is there anything else we can do?" Katherine asked as Brother Morely turned to leave.

"Just keep him quiet and pray. I'll be praying for him too." Then he placed his top hat on his head—an unusual hat for the trail—and trudged away through the mud, bending his head low to avoid the rain drizzling on his face.

"He'll get better, Katherine," said Nathanial, placing his hand on her shoulder. "Try not to worry."

Katherine dropped to the floor of the wagon bed by Isaac's side, and the crying inside of her exploded into uncontrollable tears. "What can I do? What can I do?" she repeated over and over again.

Hesitantly at first, Nathanial took Katherine into his arms. He held her tight and then, as she continued sobbing, he began wiping the tears from her face with his hand. "It's all right. He'll be all right, Kate. We'll take care of him day and night, and he will get better. I'm sure of it, Kate. I'm sure of it."

Taking a deep breath to control herself, Katherine looked up into Nathanial's eyes, and they calmed her. "How can you be so sure?" she asked between sobs.

"I don't know. But I am. He'll get better."

Somehow peace filled Katherine's heart and washed over her, and she believed him.

"Mama," Isaac murmured.

"Yes, Isaac, I'm right here," she replied, wiping the tears from her chin. She again placed her hand on his forehead to check his fever.

"I need some water. I'm so thirsty."

"All right, Isaac," responded Katherine. Nathanial quickly dipped water out of a covered bucket into a tin cup and handed it to Katherine. She raised Isaac's head and held the cup to his lips.

"Katie, dearest," whispered Maddie, "and wasn't the good doctor after saying no water, then?"

"He's not a doctor, Maddie. And even if he were, it seems a ridiculous thing to deprive someone who is burning up from the one thing that can cool the heat inside him." Isaac held the cup with both hands on top his mother's, and, though sipping very slowly, he continued drinking for some time.

"The water seems to make him feel better," said Nathanial.

"It just doesn't seem right to keep it from him," added Katherine. "I'm certain a mother receives inspiration regarding her own children. Maddie, please put the flannel shirt and the wool pants in the trunk. Isaac won't be wearing them now, but perhaps he can wear them this winter."

"Well, 'n I pray that your inspiration be comin' from heaven, dear Katherine," Maddie responded. She lifted the latch on the trunk, opened the lid, and, folding the shirt and pants, placed them neatly inside. The rain continued to drizzle.

Late in the morning, after a week of no improvement in Isaac's condition, Maddie pulled the horses to a stop to wait in line to cross the Platte. The river, about a quarter of a mile wide, rolled unusually fast, deep, and muddy brown.

A driver of a wagon team at the edge of the river cracked his reins against the backs of his oxen. "Get up!" he yelled and whistled repeatedly. But the oxen, fearing the strange water, refused to pull forward. Inside the wagon bed, a woman and her three little boys sat high on top of trunks, crates, and bags stacked to lift the supplies and the mother and her children above the waters of the Platte. The family held tightly to one another.

On the land a clattering crowd of men, women, and children bustled here and there with their arms full. They too stacked their goods in their wagons, placing bedding, clothing, and perishable foods at the very top, in an attempt to keep them dry.

Nathanial neared Katherine's wagon. "How's Isaac now, Kate?" he asked. "When I left at sunup, he was asleep, and Maddie said she'd care for him."

"He's about the same, Nathanial. Thank you for your help during the night. I must have been terribly exhausted when you came. I fell into such a deep sleep that I never awoke as I had planned so that you might go and sleep too."

"I'm glad I stayed," he responded. "You look better, as if you might have finally gotten a little rest."

"You've probably stayed up all night with him just as many nights as I have—if not more. It is you who needs sleep."

"I'm worried, though, Nathanial," added Katherine. "Isaac hardly talks at all now."

Nathanial swallowed hard. "He's weak, Kate. The others who have had it have gone through the same—kind of a delirium."

"Nathanial, I have to ask you for something."

"Anything, Kate. You know you can ask me for anything."

"Will you give Isaac a blessing? The Lord knows what I've been through. I really believe it is His will that Isaac should live. And I know you believe it too. I trust you, Nathanial," she said with tears filling her eyes. "Could you give Isaac a blessing? Will you ask the Lord to let him live?"

He took his hat into both of his hands. "I'll do my best, Kate."

Katherine and Nathanial climbed into the wagon, and Maddie looked up at them, worry etched in her eyes and lined in her face. She held a wet cloth to Isaac's forehead. "The fever 'tis burning that high, the water turns hot on the cloth almost the moment you lay it on, it does."

"We'll need another elder," said Nathanial.

"Look," said Katherine, pointing out the wagon. "Amos Taggart. He's coming our direction. We can ask him to help."

"That one, Katie? He's the one I'm after warnin' you about. Are you sure, then?"

"He's an elder in good standing, Maddie."

"Amos!" Nathanial called to Brother Taggart

Stopping, but staying clear of the wagon, Amos responded. "Yes, Nathanial?"

"Isaac is quite sick and—"

Amos interrupted. "I heard he was sick. The cholera, isn't it?"

"It looks to be. He's been burning with fever for a week now. Could you help us administer a blessing?"

"I would, Nathanial," he responded, averting his eyes. "You know I would. But my mother is with me. She's getting on in years now, and has no one else to care for her. If something should happen to me, I don't know who would help her to finish the trek and how she could possibly get along on her own in the Salt Lake Valley. You understand. This sickness passes from one to the next like flies to milk."

Nathanial's eyes grew wide in disbelief. It took him a moment to respond. "You'd better get on quickly, then, *Brother Taggart*," he finally said with an exaggerated emphasis on the word "brother." "Perhaps you can find a less sickly 'one of the least of these' to assist."

At a loss for an adequate reply, Amos simply tipped his hat and continued on, the forced smile on his face leading the way.

"Aye, the boy turns me thick! If 'n I weren't only half his size and past me prime, I'd be givin' him who-began-it. What and wasn't I after tellin' you there, Katherine McBride, about that Kildarian weasel?" commented Maddie, still seated at the buckboard.

"Shh, Maddie, he'll hear you," cautioned Katherine.

"Well, 'n do you think Madeline McFarland should care at all, at all? Let 'em hear from this forsaken spot to Ireland and back. A weasel's a weasel, no matter how soft ye say it."

"I'll get Sam," said Nathanial.

The rain slowed to a sprinkle and then to a stop as Katherine and Maddie waited. Through a cloudy haze, the sun burned gradually more brightly, and cottonwood trees lining the banks of the river swayed and dripped pacifying drops upon the river below them. But the water continued to rage.

Katherine and Maddie watched as the wagon whose driver had experienced great difficulty in getting the oxen to enter the water now appeared to float more than roll. It was midway across the Platte now. The oxen tilted their heads up and moved slowly forward, their backs only a few inches above the water. While the family inside the wagon struggled to keep balance and to keep each other inside, the river slapped heavily against the sides of the wagon and sent sprays up over the top. Katherine forgot to breathe until after she saw the oxen struggle up the bank of the river and, only under the lashing of the driver's whip, heave the wagon out of the water and up onto land.

Soon Nathanial arrived with Sam, and Sam anointed Isaac's head with oil. They then placed their hands on his head as Maddie looked on from out the back of the wagon. Katherine, hopeful and expectant, knelt by Isaac, who was asleep, and then bowed her head.

"By the authority of the Melchizedek Priesthood, through our Lord and Savior Jesus Christ, we give you this blessing, Isaac," began Nathanial, taking a deep breath. "And . . . and if it be the will of the Lord, let Him . . . let Him take me in your place." Katherine looked up at Nathanial and placed her hand on his arm as though to stop him. He continued, however: "For your mother loves you deeply, Isaac, and has lost much already."

Nathanial paused then as if waiting for the words to come to him and, after what seemed a minute or two, went on. "The Lord loves you and your mother very much," he continued. "Things have been difficult for the two of you, but his angels are assisting you, and your suffering shall be counted to you as a blessing. He expects great things of you, Isaac, and of your descendants through generations. Therefore, Isaac, we bless you that by the healing power of Jesus Christ, this illness will run its course and leave your body. You will become whole and strong again, able to assist your mother now and through the rest of her life.

"You will go to Zion, and there you will grow into an adult and marry in the house of God and raise a family up unto the Lord. We seal these blessings upon you in the name of our Savior, Jesus Christ. Amen."

By the time Nathanial was finished, tears streamed down Katherine's face. "Thank you, Sam and Nathanial," said Katherine. "Your blessing is a great relief to me. He will get well now." She smiled. "I know he will."

"Amen and amen," whispered Maddie, after a quiet pause. "Gentlemen, would to God your prayer is heard and locked in heaven." Through tears, which were unusual for her, Maddie added, "And 'tis little Isaac here that is all I'll know of Michael again upon this earth."

Leaning out of the wagon, Katherine embraced Madeline. "Before you know it, Maddie, we'll all be together in our home in Zion. With Isaac. He'll be running all over the country exploring, and we'll have a hard time keeping up with him. You'll see. I just know it to be true."

"In faith, I'll be believ'n' now because you believe, Katie, dear. And sure as Ireland is itself me home, if the Lord hears prayers at all, he'll be hearin' this prayer today, 'tis sure. A million thanks to ye Mr. Atkinson and Mr. Brighton."

"Sam," Katherine said as she held Isaac's hand, "how is Sarah today? Is she getting any closer?"

"I believe so, Katherine. She complained for the last twenty miles about the unsteadiness of the wagon. It can't be long now. We'll be lucky to get Sarah across the river before her true labor starts."

Sam put on his hat to leave.

"We'll be back when it's your turn to cross," said Nathanial. "We'll bring a couple more men."

"Thank you. Thank you both," Katherine responded gratefully.

The two men trudged away, their shoes slopping in the huge, muddy mess of the campground. When Katherine could see Nathanial no longer, she turned back inside the wagon.

Late that afternoon, after at least a dozen wagons had crossed the Platte without much incident, shouts for help were heard from the river. Old Silas Beal from the group ahead of them had fallen from his wagon where he sat at his son's side. His son, who held the reins, dared not jump in after him for fear of losing the entire wagon, which held in the back his wife and children. He threw a rope to his father and yelled to him to grab hold.

The unrelenting rolls of the water, however, quickly carried the older man out of reach of the rope. Silas's arms struggled to grab hold of a boulder or branch, but his head sunk in and out of the water. It appeared he wasn't able to swim.

As the son called to the shore for help, three men had already jumped into the water with ropes and long branches. Another man headed into the water about fifty yards downriver with one end of a rope tied to himself and the other to a large tree on the bank. Though they waded and swam as fast as they could to reach Silas, the first three men missed him. The old man's hand touched a branch held out to him, but, sinking in and out of the water as he did, he could not see well enough to grasp the branch securely.

By the time the river swept him near the last man waiting down river, Silas was under water completely. Though the rescuer positioned himself at the center of the river, directly in the old man's path, he could not find Silas, even after plunging many times under the surface of the river. It was simply too deep, too muddy, and too fast. Silas was gone.

A solemn hush pervaded the camp from one end to the other. Only the cottonwood trees creaked in their heavy sway. Katherine stood by the river, tears running down her face. A scripture came to her mind, one from the book of Isaiah: "And his heart was moved, and the heart of his people, as the trees of the wood are moved with the wind."[4]

Why, Lord? Why must it be? Have we all not suffered enough?

Learned enough? Are we not all now in the depths of humility?

"Kate." It was Nathanial. The sound of his footsteps had been silenced by the rushing of the river. "We'll get through this, Kate. Somehow—with the help of God—we'll get to Zion, and we'll get on with our lives. For some reason this is all part of His plan, and one day we'll know why."

Katherine continued to look at the river, at the place where she'd last seen Silas. She remained quiet, afraid that if she spoke, she might not be able to control her crying.

Wrapping his arm gently around Katherine's shoulder, Nathanial walked her back to the wagon.

In a meeting that night with the company captains, Jeb Hutchings declared that, though it was dangerous to delay their westward progress because of possible early winter snow in the mountains ahead, it would be best to camp at the river until a raft could be constructed to ferry the wagons across. Trees were plentiful. If the men all worked together, a buoyant, sturdy raft could be constructed in less than a week, perhaps in only three or four days.

The next morning, as the slamming of axes and shouts of "timber!" echoed over and over again at the outskirts of the camp, Isaac opened his eyes and called for his mother. His fever was gone.

"You slept a very long time, Isaac," said Katherine, perhaps happier than she had ever been. Quickly, she brought a cup of water to him and held it to his lips.

Isaac took two or three little sips. "I dreamed I was with Papa," said Isaac weakly. "He told me to take care of you."

Katherine's eyes widened. "You saw Daddy?" she questioned. "You spoke with him? What . . . what did he look like?"

"Just like he always did, Mama," answered Isaac simply, his words slow and softly spoken. "But he was dressed all in white. He smiled all the time, and we walked together in a forest filled with gigantic trees. The trunks were wider than the wagon is long." Isaac coughed. "Can I have some more water?"

"Yes, of course you can." Katherine again held the cup to Isaac's lips; his fingers trembled slightly as he held on to the cup.

Her eyes glittering with tears, Katherine asked, "Were you with him long?"

"No. Just a while. He said he couldn't stay with me much. That he was very busy but would see us soon. And he said to give you a message from him. Something about a door." Isaac coughed and paused to think. "I know. Papa said to tell you that there is someone at the door and you must say hello. "

"That's how Papa and I met!" exclaimed Katherine. "I answered the door, and he was there. And I forgot to say hello."

"He said you must listen to the Spirit of God. And . . . and he said you must let him go, Mama."

Though Katherine had thought that after all the crying she had done in the past few days, she had no tears left, her tears now streamed in torrents, and Isaac's face became a blur.

"Maddie, Maddie!" she called out excitedly, turning her eyes to a fuzzy silhouette of Maddie against the sunshine as it poured in through the front of the wagon. "Isaac is better! He's talking, and his fever is gone! And Maddie," Katherine added as her friend came closer, "he has dreamed of Michael."

Katherine, then turning back to Isaac, hugged him tightly and whispered, "I love you from here to the Milky Way and back."

"As big as the sun," said Isaac, closing his eyes.

"Well, 'n praise be to our God in His heaven," exclaimed Maddie after checking Isaac's temperature and placing her hands wide on her hips. "Our little bairn is back wi' us."

A short while later, Katherine fed Isaac a little warm corn-meal gruel she had sweetened with their last bit of honey. Then, with a smile that almost floated on her face, she took a stiff brush and a flat stick and began scraping the thick, dried mud off Isaac's shoes.

June 31

My Dear Friend,

Who can understand the ways of God? Yesterday the river took Silas Beal back home to his Father in Heaven. Today the Lord brings my son back home to me. Why would he choose to take one and leave the other?

The why's and wherefore's, I do not know. But I feel His love deeply. I feel His care, His constancy, and His abiding love. Trust and faith in Him are so very important. His love is there for us all. It's there for you. I know it is as I know I live.

Love,
Katherine

Thirteen

On the afternoon of the seventh day, as Katie and her family headed east through a mountain pass, sets of billowy clouds lined the entire horizon. Much like enormous, prehistoric animals making ready for a race or a charge, each billow seemed like a separate species. Darkened underbellies lay immobile under gigantic, floating heads, jagged puffs of ears, and coats of rolling cotton. Cloud heads reared to the left and to the right as if neighing or snorting in impatience. Even if the company turned around and ran, there would still be no escape.

Quickly, darkness spread across the sky directly above them until the sun became imprisoned. As heavy, scattered droplets began to fall, thunder rolled along the tops of the mountains, and flashes of light sporadically lit the blackened sky. Katie counted the seconds between each flash of light or strike of lightning and the successive crash of thunder. When she could not count to two after a huge lightning bolt struck behind a hill in the distance, Katie's eyes grew wide, and she stopped in her tracks.

"Let's take cover!" yelled Pa as he pointed to a rocky ravine that sloped down to the left of them.

"Wait! Let's catch up to the carts ahead of us. They're probably waiting for us in a safe place!" cried Micah.

"No time, Micah. They're too far ahead of us. Follow me! Let's move!"

Scrambling down the rocks in order to position himself to

help the others, he stretched out his arms to assist Ma first and then to help each of them step carefully through the jagged rocks. Pa, having to shout now to be heard above the rain and bursts of thunder, then called, "Split up and take cover under the boulders!"

"Why do we have to split up?" yelled Lindsay. "Let's stick together!"

"No, we can't!" Pa shouted back. His voice could barely be heard now. "We won't fit in the rocks! And if lightning strikes . . . if lightning strikes us, we won't all be hit together."

Lindsay started crying.

"Morgan!" Pa called, an eerily bright crack of light suddenly illuminating all of them. For an instant there was the illusion of everyone being petrified, motionless in time and storm. They looked at each other in silence.

Pa called again, "Morgan! Take Lindsay with you! Go! All of you!"

The family moved as quickly as possible along the rocks at the bottom of the ravine toward the huge boulders—some seven and eight feet tall—that walled it. Pa pointed to several hollows and motioned to his family to take cover there.

Making her way at the back of the group, her hair and clothing drenched with rain, Katie stopped and turned to look at the blackened sky. Then, before continuing on, she caught a movement by a lone boulder about a hundred yards back at the center of the ravine. It was Micah, fallen to the floor of the wash. Though her mouth moved as she cried out, obviously in tears, she could not be heard above the storm. She held her ankle in her hands. Katie called for help, but her words were blown back to her along with the sheets of rain.

An elongated, thick jag of lightning streaked from the top of the sky to the low horizon, and Micah's figure appeared clear and bright. Micah looked much like Katie's mother—the same close-to-translucent blonde hair; slender, long arms and legs; and even the same hollows in her cheeks.

With strikes of lightning and blasts of thunder simultaneous,

Katie turned back for Micah. The rocks were becoming more slippery and difficult to traverse. And it was uphill. Eventually, however, Katie reached her.

"My ankle!" called out Micah when Katie was close enough to hear. "I fell, and I think it's broken!"

Kneeling down to look at Micah's ankle, Katie decided that if the ankle were broken, it wasn't a bad break. Though scraped and bloody, the ankle was not swollen, and no bones were sticking out.

"Hold on to me!" cried Katie through the thunder. "We have to take cover!"

Pulling Micah up and onto her good leg, Katie held her right arm around Micah's waist while Micah wrapped her left arm around Katie's shoulders. In this manner, the girls slowly made progress, Micah balancing herself with her injured limb as she maintained most of her weight on the good leg.

"There!" called Katie as she pointed Micah toward what looked to be a small cave formed by fallen rock. The space turned out to be almost big enough for the two of them, Katie's side exposed to the cold rain by about an inch. They were squished as tightly as they could be. It made no sense, though, to continue on to search for a better spot. The rain had now turned to soft hail, and the lightning did not seem to be lessening.

Rain dripped through the rocks above them, especially onto Micah's legs. "I'm really cold," said Micah.

"The storm will be over soon," Katie replied. "It can't last forever."

Just then a gigantic column of light, accompanied by a deafening explosion, hit across the ravine. The girls and the rocks around them turned momentarily white. Clapping her hands quickly to her ears, Micah moaned.

"Is everyone all right?" Pa called from what seemed a mile away. Following the direction of each successive voice that called out, "We're okay," Katie's eyes darted down the ravine to the left and then to the right.

After a brief silence, Katie called out, "Micah hurt her ankle!"

"Is she all right?" asked Pa.

Katie looked at Micah. "Yes," she answered. "She's okay!"

"All right. Hang in there, girls! We'll be out of this soon!" Pa replied.

"I'm so cold," said Micah to Katie, and then again she repeated, "I'm really, really cold." Her teeth chattered, and her lips were blue.

Katie took off her jacket and wrapped it around Micah. Though the outside was wet, the inside was dry and somewhat warm.

"I think I'm going to throw up. I feel . . . I feel really sick," Micah said in a voice growing ever fainter.

Katie knew very little about first aid, but she had heard something about shock. "Put your head down, Micah. As far as you can." Katie guided Micah's head down, but there was no room to raise Micah's legs up.

"Is that any better?" asked Katie.

"What?" asked Micah, either unable to hear through the thunder and hail or too disoriented to understand.

"I said, are you feeling better now?"

"I think so. A little. But I'm so cold."

Picking up a flat rock that lay at her feet, Katie held it above Micah's head to deflect the drops of water that had been landing on Micah's legs. Katie held the rock for many minutes, her hand eventually feeling as if it had frozen into ice.

"Can we say a prayer?" Micah asked.

"A prayer?" Katie didn't know what to say. Her knowledge of how to pray was about the same as her knowledge of calculus or trigonometry—zero. "I guess," she replied finally. A little afraid that Micah might faint, or worse, fall into a shock-related coma, Katie thought a prayer certainly couldn't hurt. "You say it, though," Katie said.

"Okay," replied Micah so softly that Katie could barely hear, even though they were so close. Micah bowed her head, so Katie did the same.

"Father in Heaven," Micah began. She spoke slowly, catching

a short breath after every two or three words. "I know I'm not always like I should be. I know I have a long way to go. But I know you can make me feel better and stop the lightning so that we can get through this. And I know you sent Katie to help me. I don't know why. I don't deserve it." Here Micah's tears began flowing into the rainwater that already wet her face. "But I promise . . . I promise I'll be better. In the name of Jesus Christ, amen."

Micah raised her head and looked at Katie. "Thanks, Katie. You saved my life. I'll never forget it."

"Anyone would have helped you," replied Katie, a little embarrassed. "I couldn't just leave you there like a drenched rat stuck in the rocks, could I?"

"But I've been so . . . well, I haven't been very—"

"Listen!" Katie interrupted. "Do you hear that? The thunder is softer—it's further away! And the clouds are lifting. Do you see? Look! It's getting brighter. What a coincidence! You pray, and the storm stops."

Katie counted to four between the next lightning strike and the soft thunder that followed. Then, though it was still raining, the lightning storm could only be heard in the far distance.

"We're home free, I think!" called out Pa. You could hear the smile on his face. Quickly he was there next to Katie. "Let's see the damage," he said to Micah.

Katie climbed out of the cave, and, bending down, Pa gently felt Micah's injured ankle. "Well, not too bad at all!" Pa declared. But his smile was more of a grimace. "It'll need some attention, though. We have some first aid items in the cart. They'll do until we can get you to the medical people on up the trail. How are you feeling, Micah?" asked Pa.

"Better," she answered. "I don't feel like throwing up anymore. I still feel kind of dizzy, though."

"Well, hold on tight, 'cause you're goin' for a ride!"

Turning his back to Micah, Pa pulled her arms around his neck and helped to wrap her legs around his waist, piggyback style.

Good thing for our bloomers, thought Katie.

❦

As she sat with the others in camp that night, Katie felt different; somehow her body felt lighter, her vision sharper. She even felt taller. She couldn't exactly define the "why" of it. Perhaps, though—just maybe—she was worth something to someone.

An elderly woman dressed as a pioneer stood at the top of an incline and spoke to the huge group of pioneer youth who sat on blankets spread out below the stars. As Katie listened to the speaker, her ears and mind were also open to the new sensation of well-being that lifted her. More acutely she heard the intermittent noises around her; she felt them as somehow a part of herself: the two girls behind her who sometimes whispered, Morgan plucking at the grass near his feet, an occasional cough from a boy several yards back, a breeze blowing through the cottonwood grove at the base of the hill.

"In the past few days many of you have experienced hardships on this trek," said the speaker. "Perhaps now you can understand to some extent the depth of the sacrifice and suffering of our pioneer ancestors. My own great-grandmother, Elizabeth Jackson, watched her husband, my great-grandfather, Aaron Jackson, die from mountain fever and exposure to the cold while crossing with the Martin Handcart Company. One night, after he was too weak to swallow any of the food rations allotted to him that night—and they were down to very little, less than half a pound of flour per day and nothing else—Elizabeth woke to the bitter cold. Bedding was very scarce because they had been forced to get rid of most of the blankets to lighten the load. They were becoming too weak to pull their handcarts. Elizabeth awoke and listened for her husband's breathing. She heard nothing. She placed her hand on his body and discovered that he was dead, cold and rigid. No one had the ability to help her in the dark and freezing cold. She wrote that on that night she could not sleep, 'only watch and wait and pray for the dawn.' The next day all they could do was place him in a pile with thirteen others who had passed away in the night and shovel snow on top of the bodies. The ground was too frozen to dig a grave.

"Two nights later Elizabeth sat all night long on a rock with one of her children on her lap and one on each side of her. There was no one left in camp who was strong enough to pitch the tents. But as Elizabeth slept on that rock, her husband appeared to her in a dream. He said, 'Cheer up, Elizabeth, deliverance is at hand.' And sure enough, the next day part of a relief company sent by Brigham Young to rescue them galloped into camp. And through it all, she never lost her faith in the Lord. Her greatest hope was that their experience would inspire others to stand firm and faithful.[5]

"In her journal Elizabeth wrote:

"'I have a desire to leave a record of those scenes and events, through which I have passed, that my children, down to my latest posterity, may read what their ancestors were willing to suffer, patiently, for the gospel's sake. And I wish them to understand too that what I now word is the history of hundreds of others, who have passed through like scenes for the same cause. I also desire them to know that it was through obedience to the true and living God, and with assurance of an eternal reward—an exaltation in his kingdom—that we suffered these things. I hope too that it will inspire my posterity with fortitude to stand firm and faithful to the truth and be willing to suffer and sacrifice all things they may be required to pass through for the sake of the kingdom of God.'[6]

"I hope . . ." said the old woman. "I hope . . ." It was difficult, though, for her to continue. Her voice, already frail, cracked with emotion. Even the microphone clipped to her neckline could not capture and amplify her broken words. Finally her voice evened and strengthened, and Katie could understand.

"The small sacrifices I have made in my lifetime do not compare to her suffering. But I know I have lived my life with greater courage and with greater faith because of her. And I thank her for that. I hope to be able to embrace her and tell her these words face-to-face when my time here is over." Her voice again faltering with emotion and fatigue, the woman could not continue and ended abruptly, only adding an affirmation that her words were said in the name of Jesus Christ.

A new, bold idea occurred to Katie: *I could do that. I think I could do that. If I believed God wanted me to cross the plains, to keep trying even though it was freezing and others were dying around me, if I really believed, I think I could do it. I've made myself do many things these past few days that I never thought I could do. And I didn't do them for me.*

Then her mother's face, pale, drunken, and exhausted, loomed over Katie's thoughts. "You're just like your Dad, Katie," the face said. "You're weak. You're a quitter just like him. Just like him. Just like me." And then the face drew back as it guzzled a bottle of liquor.

It's true, thought Katie. *I've never faced a challenge head-on in my life. I'm a quitter. How can I be someone if I fail at everything? I fail at school. I fail with my friends. Even my own dad didn't think I was good enough to stick around for.* She turned her face away from those seated by her and looked instead to her side, directly into the night breeze. Tears blew across Katie's eyes and dried themselves in her hair.

"Are you okay, Katie?" asked Ma later that evening as Katie sat reading the old journal by the light of the campfire. "I thought you looked upset tonight after Sister Jackson spoke to us."

Katie was surprised. She didn't think anyone had noticed. Not knowing what to say, Katie said nothing.

"You know what I like about you?" Ma asked after a short wait. "First, I like your sense of humor. You make everyone laugh, even when we're all sweaty and exhausted. What I like about you the most, though, is that you care. And you prove it. You could have let go of the cart when it was slipping down the hillside. But you didn't. You cared what would happen to the rest of us. And you could have left Micah where she was. Someone would have realized eventually that she was missing. Or you could have sent someone else to go back for her. But you didn't. You did it. You went back. You have a great deal of courage, Katie. And you care. I think out of everyone I have come to know on this trek, it's you I admire the most."

Katie looked up, not sure whether she could dare to believe or to trust. "We've met before," said Katie simply. "About six years ago. I was ten years old."

Ma's eyes narrowed and deepened as she looked at Katie and tried to recall the connection. "You looked very familiar to me when I first saw you. But I couldn't remember where I had seen you before."

"It was in the bathroom at the church. I was retying my hair. You said . . ." And then Katie looked straight into Ma's concerned face. "You said you didn't like to get anywhere near my mother."

"I remember you now—I can see that little girl in you," said Ma, tears welling up in her eyes even before she spoke. "And then I never saw your mother at church again. I'm so sorry, Katie. Can you believe me when I say I've regretted those words ever since?"

"I asked for your address and went over to your house the next day to apologize," she continued. "Did your mother tell you? I think she said you were at a friend's house."

Katie shook her head slowly. "No," she replied. "She never told me."

"I didn't know what to say. So I just told her I was sorry and that I hoped I could come back and apologize to you too." Then Ma chose her words carefully. "She told me I wasn't welcome in her home and to never come back. She said she would call the police if she ever saw me near you again. She was really angry. I just cried; I didn't know what I could do.

"I brought a plate of chocolate chip cookies over to your house and tried to give them to your mother. I had written a note and placed it on the plate. Your mother wouldn't accept the cookies. She said that I had probably poisoned them. Then your mother made it very clear that I was to never come near the house again. I left the note on the doorstep.

"She wouldn't let the bishop talk with her either. I realized there was nothing I could do to change my mistake. I know I'm the reason your mother and you never came back to church. I've lived with it ever since."

Katie looked thoughtful, but she said nothing in reply.

"I decided that day I would never criticize anyone ever again in my life," Ma continued. "And I've tried to keep that promise, for six years now."

Still Katie was silent.

"I would give a lot to be able to erase what I said that day. There are a lot of things I would like to erase that I've done in my life."

Ma dared to touch Katie on the arm. "Katie," she said. "Look at me."

Katie looked up. The tears were sliding down Ma's face now. "Have you ever done anything in your life that you wish you could undo?"

"Just my whole life," Katie said after a pause. "I'd like to do my entire life over again."

"Then you understand," said Ma. "Sometimes I want to be so right and do so much good in life that it hurts inside. It hurts because I know I'll never be perfect. We can't be. But that's why we have Christ. We can learn from our mistakes and progress because His redemption rescues us—if we let it—from each of those mistakes. But we have to let go of them. He said, 'Come unto me, all ye that labour and are heavy laden, and I will give you rest.'[7] It's my favorite scripture."

A strange feeling then enveloped Katie. It was an over-whelmingly warm and sweet feeling that brought tears to her eyes—like warm maple syrup or molasses pouring through her.

Ma had stopped talking. Picking up a half-charred stick that lay at their feet, she began tracing patterns in the dirt with the blackened end. "Will you forgive me, Katie, for those words I said six years ago? It was the stupidest thing I've ever done."

Christ. Mistakes. Redemption. Will you forgive me? The extraordinary feeling that told her what? It was all too much to make sense of right now. "I think I better go to my tent and get some sleep," Katie answered without really answering.

"Of course," said Ma. She stood up slowly and dropped the charred stick back into the fire. "I'll see you in the morning."

By herself again, still at the campfire, Katie turned on her flashlight and opened the journal to finish the page she had been reading. There was little light left from the fire. The flames were sparse and sputtering.

Dear Friend,

Today has been a day of great trial. At times I feel such despair, and it seems as though just picking up my feet and going on takes as much effort almost as moving a mountain. But even moving a mountain is not impossible, I know, if I have enough faith. I want to be like the sego lily that grows here on the plain. It grows independent, strong, and free, just one or two white flowers by themselves, shooting up high above all the wild grasses around them. Its roots, though, are what count. The tiny bulbs withstand the cold and can even sustain life if a person is without food.

Here is what they look like!

The tiny bulbs remind me of the sustenance of faith. Faith must be solid, with—nothing wavering. I must have faith in my Savior, concentrate only on the hour ahead and cast my burdens upon him. There I shall find rest and comfort. For he said, 'Come unto me, all ye that labour and are heavy laden, and I will give you rest.' "

Goosebumps breezed over Katie's skin as she recognized this scripture in Katherine's journal as identical to the scripture Ma had just quoted. What were the chances of that?

Closing the journal slowly, Katie walked back to her tent, her mind swirling in thoughts. She lay in her sleeping bag for quite some time before her eyes finally closed.

Fourteen

July 7

Dear Friend,

We all knew when we began this journey to Zion that there would be much risk. Somehow, though, we never imagine the severity of future suffering until it is actually upon us. Many have become ill with cholera, like Isaac had, or too weak to walk from hunger and fatigue. The men especially are worn and spent. Rations are being reduced weekly, and often the men go without to give to their wives and children. The men by turn keep watch at night and then drive the teams or walk by day.

Little Joseph Magelby has never recovered from his illness and his fall from the wagon but has only grown worse. We heard sad news this morning. Joseph is not expected to live much longer.

I knew our calling to go West was divine. I had no doubts. I knew it more than anything I've known in my life. I thought then that our God would protect us. "Why must this suffering be, dear friend?" I ask our Father in Heaven often. His answer, though, is never direct.

His answer, to me at least, is in little miracles, little miracles that let me know He is there, not only standing by us but stretching forth His hand in our behalf. The answer is *in the dream Isaac had of Michael and in His response to my prayer for Isaac to be made well. The answer is Maddie finding us over long distances of ocean, land, and time. It's in the warmth that spreads over my heart when I read the words of Christ and in the smile that spreads across my face when I awake to a beautiful new morning.*

I believe His answer is, "Trust in Me."

"Katherine! Katherine, come quickly!" called out John Jamison. "Sarah's having her baby!"

"Isaac! Maddie! I'll be gone awhile," Katherine called out to them as she hastily closed her ink bottle and placed it and the pen in their box. "If you need me, I'll be with Sarah. I'm sure the company will not move out until her baby is safely delivered."

Maddie clapped her hands, and they landed softly together. "We're havin' a wee babe then!"

"Yes, Maddie. We're having a baby!" repeated Katherine, grasping Maddie's hands in hers excitedly.

"Isaac, you stay close to Maddie, please. No horned-toad hunting while I'm gone," Katherine ordered as she wrapped her shawl around her shoulders. The mornings were often chilly.

"Yes, ma'am," answered Isaac as he kissed his mother on the cheek.

Running all the way, her ankle boots and the hem of her skirt scraping through the brush, Katherine arrived out of breath at Sarah's wagon.

"How is she?" Katherine asked Sam, who stood outside the wagon, his hat scrunched in his hands. Supplies were stacked on the ground near him to make more room inside.

"She's not doing very well, Katherine. The baby is breech, and the midwife has not been able to turn it around. Sarah is getting very weak and dizzy; the midwife is afraid she might faint."

"Did you give Sarah a blessing, Sam?"

"We did early this morning."

"May I?" Katherine asked, turning toward the curtain at the back of the wagon.

"Of course, Katherine. I would have let you know sooner, but her water broke at about two o'clock in the morning, and the midwife said she had many hours to go," explained Sam as he helped Katherine up into the wagon.

Inside, Sarah lay still for the moment, her eyes closed and her head turned to the side. Her face appeared almost as white as the pillow sheet next to her.

"Sarah," Katherine spoke softly as she took her hand. "It's me, Katherine."

"Katherine?" Sarah responded weakly, her eyes only opening halfway. "What shall we do? My little Jacob Wheeler doesn't seem to want to be born."

Katherine said nothing for a moment. She looked at Sadie, the midwife. There were no answers there. She looked at Sarah's round stomach and then searched in Sarah's tired eyes.

"We'll wait, Sarah. And trust in the Lord. You'll see. He will not fail us."

Sarah's eyes filled with tears. "But, Katherine," she said. "He took our baby Ann home to him. I prayed so hard that He would make her well. Perhaps it is not His will that Jacob should stay with us either."

"Shh," responded Katherine, holding her finger to Sarah's lips. "We must have hope."

The events leading to the death of Sarah's little Ann often lingered near Katherine's mind, but she tried not to let herself think of them. First, there had been a mob of angry men—some said there were up to nine hundred of them—camped out near Carthage, lying in wait to attack Nauvoo. In September they marched into the city, settling into an abandoned farm on the outskirts. From there, they sent cannonballs soaring in. Mobs of men lorded over the streets of Nauvoo, ordering families to get out. Rampaging from house to house, some of the mobs plundered livestock and whatever else they could find. They destroyed what they could not steal, even tearing up floor-boards. The sick were cruelly treated, as were those mourning their dead. The women and children fled across the river, many of them taking nothing with them. Sarah escaped with baby Ann while Sam stayed to defend the city and those who could not run.

The baby, already sick with a mild pneumonia, died during the cold of the night in the makeshift tent Sarah shared with another family.

Sarah now turned her head away from Katherine and bit her lip. Another contraction was beginning. "Don't push yet, Sarah," instructed the midwife. "The baby is still not in position. Try to relax."

Sarah's eyes grew wide, and she began to gasp. "I can't!" she cried as she tried desperately to get enough air. "I can't do this anymore. It hurts too much. I . . . I can't anymore!" she yelled.

"She's panicking," said the midwife. "Try to relax, Sarah. You need to stay calm."

"Sarah," Katherine said forcefully. "Take a deep breath. And another. Just let go and let yourself feel the pain. Think of the pain turning the baby around. Think that if you relax, the baby can turn."

Sarah closed her eyes and took several deep breaths, blow-ing out each respiration through pursed lips. She grabbed Katherine's hand. Then, after a minute or two, she breathed out, "The pain's gone now." And tears ran down her cheeks.

Katherine placed her hands on Sarah's stomach, with Sar-ah's hand still gripping hers, and then Katherine bowed her head to their hands. After a few moments, something happened. The baby moved, stopped, and then moved again. Lumps, big and small, pushed, swung and plunged in every direction under the skin of Sarah's bulging stomach.

"The baby's changing position!" exclaimed Sarah, smiling through her tears.

Three times the baby moved radically as Katherine felt its shape slide down, freeing Sarah's ribs.

"I see the baby's head!" cried out Sadie. "Next time, push, Sarah! Push as hard as you can!"

The next contraction came quickly, and with only two pushes, the baby was free. And so was Sarah.

"It's a boy!" called Sadie, though it was clear for all to see. Sam opened the curtain and laughed in relief. And then the baby cried, loud and strong, and Sadie, wrapping him quickly in Sarah's homespun blanket, placed him on his mother's chest and into her arms.

⁓⁕⁓

That afternoon, as the wagon train followed the Platte River and Katherine's horses plodded slowly along, Isaac named rock formations that protruded from small hills lining the trail.

"This one will be Great Buffalo Droppings," he announced, laughing loudly. "And you see that one in back of this hill? That is the Great Buffalo Dung Dropper! The most gigantic buffalo that ever there was on earth!"

"Let's stick to happy comparisons," responded Katherine, seated with Isaac and Maddie at the buckboard and trying very hard not to laugh. "Let's not let our minds wallow in buffalo dung."

"Whyever not, me lady?" Maddie protested as she drove the team of horses. "Aye, and aren't you after readin' Shakespeare?" Then with a deep, rolling brogue, Maddie recited: "'A r-r-r-rose by any other name would smell as sweet.' You might be callin' that formation of rock anythin' you like, Katie, but it still looks like dung, to be sure!"

"I can't argue with that, Maddie." Katherine laughed as she pulled Isaac onto her lap.

"You, sir," said Katherine to Isaac, "are in great need of a bath. I hope we stop before dark so we can dunk you a few times in the river."

"Look there, Mother. It's a giant teapot!"

At the end of one formation, a shape like a teapot, with

146

spout and ornamentation, hung ready to be poured. Katherine remembered her grandmother Devonshire's teapot, made of a fine, milky porcelain. Gilt around the edges and decorated with dainty pink roses, which her grandmother had said were hand-painted, the teapot had been brought over on the boat by Katherine's grandmother when she was just newly married.

"This teapot and its matching tea cups are all I have to remind me of my home in England," Grandmother had said to Katherine. "They belonged to my mother, and she gave them to me as a wedding gift just before we left England."

The teapot and cups held a place of honor in Grandmother Devonshire's home. Displayed on top of the china cabinet on a round silver platter, they sparkled in the light from the south-facing window. Grandmother always kept the teapot and cups gleaming, and the silver platter that held them was always polished to perfection.

On special occasions, and always on Christmas morning, Grandmother arranged the teacups carefully on the table, and the family would delight in her cranberry scones and peppermint tea. One Christmas morning, however, a few of the grandchildren, including eight-year-old Katherine, rushed to the table in a race to grab the biggest scones. Someone knocked the iron candelabra centerpiece, and it fell heavily, directly on top of Grandmother's teapot. The teapot shattered.

At least twenty pairs of eyes turned quickly to Grandmother, who stood in the kitchen doorway, her calico apron tied at her waist. No one moved or spoke.

"Well," said Grandmother after assessing the irreparable damage to her teapot. "This teapot has been a blessing in my life for a great many years now. It's time to let it go and open the way for other blessings. The Lord gives and the Lord takes away. And I've noticed his giving is always much greater than his taking."

It had been a long time since Katherine had thought of the broken teapot and her grandmother's exceptional wisdom, but now the words echoed in her mind, *It's time to let go and open the way for other blessings. The Lord gives and the Lord takes away.*

"Have you seen Nathanial today?" she asked Madeline.

"Aye, and at just about eight this mornin' he would be at the Wilson's wagon back a few, he would. He was just after givin' them a dig out with a broken wheel. Are you watching him today then, dearie?" Maddie asked with a pleased chuckle.

"No, Maddie. Nothing like that 'to be sure'—as you would say. Isaac was just hoping Nathanial would go fishing with him when we make it to the bridge. That's all."

Maddie hooted in amusement. "Away on, Katie! And do you think I came up the Foyle river in a bubble now, lass? Weren't it just yesterday you were after talkin' about him all the day long? 'And Nathanial did this,' she says, 'and Nathanial said that.' Finally in the right pot, you are, Katie, and not before time, I say! No matter if'n you thank me now or later for planting you in it."

"I'll do my own planting, thank you—wherever and whenever that may be," responded Katherine, amused.

"Aye, but sure, your lips are sealed then. 'Tis of no matter to me at all, me lady. Not at all," said Maddie as the trail wound around a dry hill into a small, grassy canyon filled with tall trees.

Inside the canyon, the quiet was immediate. The hooves of the horses landed more softly on the grass and sandy soil; Katherine, Maddie, and many others hushed their voices as they gazed in wonder at the beauty of the canyon. Running beneath a large rock arch formation, a large, riverlike stream horseshoed around the small boxed canyon. The wagons in the company ahead of them had stopped to camp, and people in their shoddy boots and dust-caked clothing climbed the arch while others swam. Cutting under the canyon walls, the water formed deep swimming holes.

Maddie pulled the horses to a stop alongside the Brightons' wagon, and Katherine, after checking to see if all was well with Sarah and Jacob, explored the canyon with Maddie and Isaac. It was not necessary to tell Isaac to take a bath; he whooped and ran to jump into the water as soon as he neared it.

"Stay on this side of the stream," Katherine called to him. It's much deeper by the canyon wall."

Isaac smiled and nodded in acknowledgment.

"We'll be needin' the soap and a towel," said Maddie as she turned back toward the wagon.

Hearing the cooing of birds, Maddie looked up the side of the canyon. Swallows and robins darted in and out of small, hidden crevices in the face of the rock. Katherine smiled and sighed at the incongruence—the peace and beauty of the water, the canyon, and the life within it and the hardship, suffering, and even death, with which they were now so familiar.

Checking first to make sure Isaac was still playing in a shallow area, Katherine knelt on the bank of a quiet, grassy bend and looked into the still water. She tucked loose strands of hair back inside her bonnet and then held still to gaze at her reflection. She looked different to herself now. Her features were, of course, still the same, though her skin was tanned more than it had ever been, but her countenance was somehow deeper, wiser, more somber, and perhaps more compassionate.

As she stared at her reflection, her heart began to warm, and the reflection softened. Was it her imagination or did she see another face now, similar to her own, but younger? The hair and eyes were dark like Katherine's own, yet the expression was full of hurt.

It is she. The thought came quickly to Katherine's heart and mind. *It is she to whom I write. What can I write that will take the hurt from her face?* Katherine looked up at the sky in search of an answer, but when she looked back, the reflection was her own again.

"I've heard it said the eyes are the mirror of the soul," commented Nathanial, standing behind her.

Startled, Katherine gasped and turned quickly. "Oh! You scared me, Nathanial. Make some noise next time you're sneaking up behind me so that I know you're coming!" She laughed.

"Sorry, Katherine. I didn't mean to surprise you," responded Nathanial with a hint of amusement in his voice. "I'm sure you didn't hear my footsteps because you were concentrating so deeply on your reflection. So what did your eyes tell you?" he asked, chuckling. "About your soul, I mean."

Katherine turned to look again at the water. "Sometimes . . . sometimes in a reflection you can see much more than you would think."

"Ah," responded Nathanial, "but that doesn't answer my question."

"Very true . . . so what do my eyes tell me about my soul? Was that it?"

"Yes, m'lady," answered Nathanial with a spark in his eye. "Come look in the water and see for yourself."

Katherine reached for his hand and pulled him down to a kneeling position beside her. She did not let go of his hand. "Well?" she asked. "What do you see?"

Nathanial gazed for a few moments at Katherine's reflection, and then he looked back for what seemed a long while into her eyes. She held her breath and waited, her eyes wet—the river-water reflection of herself more a part of her real image now. Faraway splashes, laughter, and chatter muted into an even further distance. "What I see is . . ." said Nathanial finally. "I see the deepest and most beautiful—" But here Nathanial stopped and stood abruptly, letting go of her hand.

"I . . . I can't, Kate," he said as he placed his hat back on his head.

Katherine stood up as well. "Nathanial, don't leave," she said as the tears that had filled her eyes now slid down her cheeks.

"What is it, Kate?" he asked, obviously worried. He took both her hands in his. "What's wrong? Is it Isaac?"

"Nothing is wrong." She smiled through her tears. "Nothing at all. Nathanial—well, I have something to tell you. I . . . I've been trying to fight how I feel about you for a long, long time now, Nathanial. I even tried to get rid of the Spirit that testified of it in my heart. Nathanial," she said, now looking directly into his eyes. "I love you more than I can say. I think about you all the time, and whenever I'm with you, I feel happy. I can't imagine being without you," Katherine finished, her voice intense, but a little out of breath.

Now Nathanial's eyes glossed with tears. He looked as if a thousand-pound weight had just been removed from his body. "Kate," he whispered as he touched the tears on her face and ran his fingers back through her hair. "Kate," he said again as he kissed first one eyelid and then the other. "I can't . . . I can't even tell you how I feel. Just that I love you," he said simply, his voice catching. "I love you more than my own life."

The river water that had separated their reflections then withdrew, the images in the water becoming one.

Fifteen

Katie stood on top of Rocky Ridge, a place of great hardship for many of the pioneers. She felt as if she were alone. Though some of the others were whispering, Katie heard them no more than she heard the jutting, rocky sediment around her, no more than she heard the blue of the sky. The whispers melted into the warm breeze that picked up Katie's bonnet from behind her back and lifted the dark strands of hair at the sides of her face. Gazing at the horizon, miles away, Katie felt that if she could only transport herself, she would love to lie back into the band of clouds that meshed behind a rolling line of deep blue mountains. There was no end to the mountain and no beginning to the skies. The two were impossible to separate.

The hill to the top of the ridge, mined with jutting rock slabs, reminded Katie of the Aztec temples where human sacrifices were performed. They had learned all about them in her history class last year. Mammoth steps wrapped around the hill, forming ridges to halt the roll of the handcart wheel, to split its wood—sharp ridges hidden under the snow to cut and scrape. She looked down at her feet. She wondered how they would look with rags wrapped around them instead of shoes. She imagined blood soaking through the rags, her feet blistered, cut, and frozen by the early snow and scraped by the jagged rocks.

When she was about halfway down the ridge, Katie imagined

an eleven-year-old boy, cold and weak, carrying his little brother on his back all the way up the ridge. Did he have shoes on his feet? Was his little brother crying from hunger or cold? Katie didn't know. But she could imagine. The wind might have blown just as it did now. It would have been a cold wind, though. The wind blew the snow up and into the faces of the little boys. And that made it much harder to get up the hill. The eleven-year-old boy saw others give up and fall to the rocky floor. He couldn't help them; in fact, he would have liked to join them, to rest there with them. He knew if he did, though, his little brother would freeze and die. So he kept on. He had to get his little brother into camp, safely delivered to their mother's arms.

Then Katie's eyebrows furrowed, and she bit her lip to hold back tears as she thought of what she had been told happened next. The boy arrived at camp with his little brother still on his back, and then he lay down from total exhaustion—right there to die.

Katie saw them all. They trudged up the hill with no strength left. They had been through way too much, those of the Willie Handcart Company. Too much hunger. Too much cold. Too much pushing on, pushing on, and pushing on.

Still they kept coming, she thought. *And they still trusted in God. How could that be?* Turning her teary eyes again to the blue blend of sky and mountain, Katie noticed the clouds had lifted just slightly at the center, and soft, long rays of light poured through the sky. Again she asked herself, *How could that be?* And Katie found herself wishing once more that she could believe in God as profoundly as they did.

At lunch, Katie sat with Ma on a grassy bank of the Sweetwater River. The water was deep and about fifty yards wide. It looked as if someone had purposefully laid down long stretches of grassy carpet along the banks of the river and then stuck in patches of bright green and prickly salt brush, just for effect.

Out in the grasslands, close enough that Katie could see their tails swishing, nine buffalo grazed. A sandy trail led from their pasture down to the river. Katie tried to imagine the buffalo as they once had been, thousands of them from the river to the horizon. In her imagination, though, she couldn't get rid of the many fences. Free-ranging, wild buffalo and barriers at every turn were simply not compatible.

"I don't like all of these fences," commented Katie. "There are fences everywhere! Do people really need to put them all up?"

Ma waited until she swallowed a big bite of biscuit. "That's life as we know it, I guess," she answered finally. "One reason they put up fences is to hold livestock in. But I'm sure fences show ownership as well. I know that the people who planned this trek worked for months to get permission to cross over scores of private properties. Of course, none of these fences were here when the pioneers crossed."

"It's crazy," said Katie. "Why can't land just belong to every-one? How can anyone look at a piece of the world that has been there for maybe billions of years and say, 'This is mine! Don't touch it!' It's stupid. The world can't belong to people. It doesn't seem right."

As Ma again waited to swallow before she spoke, Katie looked at her and realized something. It didn't matter anymore. What Katie had heard Ma say six years ago in the church bath-room didn't matter. Katie didn't care anymore. There were too many good things about Ma to hold that against her. Katie smiled.

"What?" asked Ma. "What are you smiling about?"

"Nothing," answered Katie. "Well . . . remember that stupid thing you did six years ago that you wished you could undo? Consider it undone."

Ma reached over to hug Katie. Holding tightly to her, Ma closed her eyes and sighed. "Thank you, Katie. Thank you."

That night was unusually black, and the campfire binding Katie and her family, lighting their encircling faces, seemed like the center of the world to her. Soft flames lapped up and around the two thick logs remaining whole while the rest of the firewood was now embers and white ash. Each of them were apparently lost in thought; no one spoke.

Katie became entranced by what appeared to be a deep burning cavern in between and under the logs. Smoldering with whitened, rocky formations, each one a distinct size and shape, the pit seemed like a tiny kingdom of its own. She could almost feel the cavern calling her inside to investigate. Katie gazed constantly upon it. *Is hell like that?* she wondered.

Once, on a Sunday radio program, Katie had heard someone speak about hell. He said it was a fiery torment of the heart and soul, a lament for the deeds of one's life and a longing to be at one with God. Katherine shuddered, the skin on her arms pricking with a sudden chill.

To be at one with God. That's what I want. And she felt that desire strongly, more strongly than she could remember feeling anything.

A faint song then began, sung simply and beautifully, like the clear sound of an Indian flute. It was Heather. No one had asked her to sing.

> *Come, come, ye Saints, no toil nor labor fear;*
> *But with joy wend your way.*
> *Though hard to you this journey may appear,*
> *Grace shall be as your day.*
>
> *'Tis better far for us to strive*
> *Our useless cares from us to drive;*
> *Do this, and joy your hearts will swell—*
> *All is well! All is well!*[8]

With her sleeve, Katie dried the tears rimming her eyes before anyone could notice them.

Later, as she lay on top of her sleeping bag—it was still too hot outside to get in it—she thought about things. Katie thought that if perhaps she could discount the bad about Ma because of all the good in her, maybe it would be possible to discount the bad in Katie herself because of the good things she was. But as she tried desperately to add to a list of perhaps two or three things she could find in herself that were good, she fell asleep.

That night Katie had a dream. She was climbing Rocky Ridge with Ma and Morgan. It was extremely cold, and Katie was very tired. She had to force herself to lift her knee up and then her foot, and then swing her foot forward. Just as they reached the top, an arrow hit Ma and then Morgan. They lay dead at her feet. As Katie turned to look at them, an arrow hit her in the back of the neck. She could feel it splitting her muscle and bone. And then she felt herself rise. But it wasn't her body that rose: her body lay down below, side by side with Ma and Morgan and ten other frozen bodies in a mass grave, covered only by snow.

Katie's spirit rose. And as she floated upward, Katie felt a great peace that reached through her entire being. "Father," she said in her dream. "I'm coming home."

And then Katie awoke. She felt loved, deeply loved. She lay still for a few moments as the unique peace and love slowly faded. Even after they were gone, Katie remained awake and for a long time as she thought about what the dream meant.

Sixteen

On the tenth day, just at first light, Katie turned to the side of her sleeping bag for Katherine's journal. Knowing that only the last entry remained, Katie had waited until she could be alone to read it. Now was a good time since everyone else was still asleep. As Katie turned to the last entry and then flipped again through the empty pages at the back to make sure she hadn't missed any writing, a heavy, folded paper fell out.

It was the painting of the Indians that Katherine had promised to complete and place in the journal! Though the years had marbled it with cracks, and paint had chipped at the fold lines, the painting was nevertheless unbelievably beautiful. How could she have captured ancient wisdom and majesty with drawn lines and paint? The colors were faded now, but Katie could imagine them as brilliant as they must have once appeared: the bright streaks of red and yellow on the Indian faces; the white, brown, and black glossy richness of the coats of the horses; the deep blue above them. The painted feathers tied to the braids of the braves and to the chief's headdress almost fluttered in the painted sky. It looked that real.

This is incredible! She really was a gifted artist—and she was my ancestor!

After examining the painting for some time, Katie folded it back up and placed it in the diary box. She then began reading the last entry.

July 8

Dearest Friend,

Our journey is more than half complete. I fear, though, that what remains shall be even more difficult than what has passed.

I saw your reflection yesterday. I do not know how. All I know is that the Lord knows you and He wants me to know you too. I saw hurt in your eyes. My dear friend, you must find the door. Windows close on our lives, but God always opens a door. We have to let some things go so that we can open the way for greater blessings. That is what my grandmother always said.

Find the door. He will be waiting on the other side. And so will I—someday.

Love,
Katherine

How strange, thought Katie. *Who does she keep writing to? Whose reflection did she see?*

Once again, Katie leafed through the pages, this time slowly and carefully. *No, there are no more entries. But she writes that her journey is only half over. Why didn't she continue to write?*

After returning the diary to its box, Katie reached deep inside her bucket and lifted out the scriptures she had been required to bring on the trek. Scraping off pieces of dirt and dried grass that had collected on and around the book, Katie opened it and began to read. She wanted to know more about the God Katherine had such complete faith in, the God in Katie's dream—the father to whom she had said with great peace, "I'm coming home."

That day, and each successive day, Katie continued reading at the place where she'd left off, almost every time the group stopped to rest. There was something about the scriptures. A sweetness, a completeness, perhaps. Something that, though she tried, she couldn't name.

Today's trek turned out to be particularly strenuous. Wanting the handcart groups to reach Martin's Cove before dark, the horseback-riding guides often rode alongside Katie's group, encouraging them to keep a fast pace. Pa's cart family still trailed behind by a substantial distance at the end of the caravan.

Stops for rest were short and long in coming, and Katie found herself very much disliking having to put down her scriptures each time it seemed she had just begun reading.

"You don't look very happy to shut those scriptures," said Morgan to Katie as he reached his hand out to help her up off the ground. "I don't know," Morgan continued. "You might just be getting a little too good for the rest of us. When you get to heaven, would you slip in a good word for me? You know—make me shine." Then putting his arm around her shoulders and winking, he added, "If that doesn't work, maybe you could snatch a halo and throw it down to me in, in . . . well, in wherever I am. And a pair of angel wings too. That way I can fly right up to where you are."

"I'd be glad to," said Katie, laughing. "There's only one problem, though. I doubt there's a halo in heaven big enough for your head! Oh, and one more problem. They'd never let someone as disgustingly full of dirt as you pass through those sparkling pearly gates."

It was true that each person only had two sets of clothing, and they had only twice been able to wash their clothes in streams and hang them to dry on the sides of the handcart. And Morgan, with a gigantic magnetlike propensity to attract dirt to himself, far outweighed the others in collected grime.

"A walking dirt clod, that's what you are!" added Katie.

"Well, then," said Morgan. And he removed his arm from Katie's shoulder, at the same time distancing himself from her by at least two yards. Katie was immediately sorry she had said anything.

After walking about twenty or thirty strides in silence, Morgan spoke. "Do you think, Katherine—that's your full name, right? Do you think that we could see each other again after this trek is over? I'll tell you a secret: you're actually my favorite trek buddy. What do you think of that?" Morgan poked her in the side with his walking stick. "I'll really miss you if I can't see you again," he added.

Katherine. How strange that he would call me Katherine, my ancestor's name. No one calls me that.

"I don't know if I'll have time," Katie teased finally. "I've been reading a lot lately, you know. And I have to take care of my mother. Besides that, I have a date already lined up for every Friday and Saturday night until the end of the year." But Katie's eyes, unusually bright and hopeful, said, "I'd love to."

"Well, then," responded Morgan, "maybe we could hang out on a Saturday morning. Breakfast at IHOP maybe. Or we could go horseback riding in the afternoon at my house. We have one horse I think you'll really like. Her name's Lady. It would be Lady Katherine and Lady. She'll like you too. I know she will."

"I've only ridden a horse once before, and I was scared to death."

"You won't be scared of Lady. She's the gentlest horse I've ever known. She . . . well, she kind of reminds me of you in that way."

Katie smiled and looked away at the mountain pass still far in front of them. They had seen it for many hours, even days, as they walked, but it never seemed to get any closer. Now it was, though. It was right there, and they were heading for the pass between two high peaks.

"Your horse doesn't buck or bite or kick, then?"

"No, she has never bucked or kicked or bitten anyone in her life," answered Morgan.

"That's good."

"It's a date, then. All right? We get back from the trek on Sunday, and we'll ride that next Saturday. You give me your phone number, and I'll call you and pick you up."

"Okay," replied Katie. But inside it wasn't just okay. Inside, there were miniature sparks of light exploding. She hadn't realized that she liked Morgan that much.

Later, as they dragged their feet and their handcart into the Martin's Cove area, the sun hung low, about midway down the sky. Instructed to leave their cart at a starting point, Pa's group began the three-mile hike into the ravine. This was the first time the eight of them had walked together without the handcart, and a cool wind at their backs pushed them along and made the climb easier. Katie felt free somehow. And she felt like she belonged, as if she could perhaps be like the others.

At the side of the pathway grew small bushes of wild roses, their blossoms so tiny that they could hardly be seen. Katie thought of a miniature rose plant that a neighbor had brought over last December as a Christmas gift for her and her mother— who knew why. Maybe the little rosebush had also been a gift to the neighbor, and she didn't like plants. In any case, it was beautiful, only ten inches high with delicate red and white roses scattered all around it. What thing of beauty, though, could survive the McBrides? Either under-watered or drenched too often, first the rosebuds had dried and petrified, and then the leaves began to mottle and fall, until nothing living appeared to remain. Katie had kept watering it, though. Just in case.

One afternoon in January, with nothing better to do, Katie had examined the plant and noticed something unusual. At the base of one branch, hidden in all the decay, two tiny light-green leaves grew, and a third leaf bud had begun to open. She noticed too that though all the other leaves and many of the branches were dead, quite a few branches still remained green at the base.

That afternoon Katie decided to operate. Hanging the plant over the trash, she picked off all of the dead leaves. Next she cut off the brown stems just until she reached where they were still green. After watering the plant well and placing the little rosebush in the sun, Katie waited and watched for several days.

On the fourth day, more leaves began to sprout, and in two month's time, the plant was healthy once again. No rosebuds had formed, though. Then, almost four months later, way past the time when Katie had given up hope, a small rose appeared. It had just begun to open when Katie left for the trek. It was white.

She thought of the plant she had saved, and it gave her hope.

Katie couldn't imagine a group of people she would rather be with. Ma was super nice and always had the right thing to say—and she trusted Katie. Zach, who was forever offering to do whatever work was needed, was possibly the smartest kid in the whole world. Micah wasn't at all like she used to be. Since Katie helped her in the storm, Micah assumed nothing. She was helpful and eager to be a good friend. Lindsay and Heather were just that—good friends. She knew she could count on them for anything. And Pa. He was everything she'd ever wanted in a dad. Morgan? Well, Morgan was *Morgan*. She had never known anyone like him.

A ravine marked by steep hills surrounding it on three sides, Martin's Cove had offered some protection from the cold, blowing winds to the suffering immigrants who had taken shelter in it many years before. There at the cove, Katie's company was divided into three groups. Each group followed a path winding around the base of the ravine as they rotated through several stations where they listened to speakers relate the experiences of the Martin, Hodgett, and Hunt Companies.

I don't think I could have waded through the Sweetwater River again either, thought Katie, as she listened at the first station. *Not after pushing my handcart through the same river days before and pushing on with my clothes soaking and then stuck stiff with the cold on my body, not after watching people die around me, not after starving for days and days. They would have had to carry me across too.*

So many, thought Katie at each station. *So many suffered so much.* She could imagine them huddling together in the snow with thin, ragged blankets, there in the ravine sitting under bare trees, on fallen logs, or at the side of bushes to protect them from the cold, blowing snow. But there wasn't anything that could really protect them. The muffled shouts of the rescuers ordering the half-frozen, almost lifeless pioneers to get up and find their own firewood because moving about might prevent them from dying, sounded in Katie's mind. She could almost see the children, too weak to even cry, their eyes wide and vacant with hunger and fear. How could they put up their tents? Most all of the men and the women had frozen feet or hands.

"On November 9," one station guide called out in a loud voice, "the violent storm ended, and the immigrants forced themselves to once again head west, even though it was recorded that some said it would be better to stay in the ravine and 'die comfortably' rather than to 'push forward into the icebound mountains.'

"On November 10, a rescuer named Ephraim Hanks met up with this group. He led a horse packed with buffalo meat for them. He wrote later that he tried to help those whose 'extremities had frozen' and who had 'lost their limbs.' He washed the damaged areas with castile soap 'until the frozen parts would fall off.' And then he would 'sever the shreds of flesh from the remaining portions of the limbs' with his scissors."

Reaching with both hands, Katie held on to her upper arms, a subconscious reflex, perhaps, to make sure her limbs were still intact. *How would it be? Such suffering—such horror. How could God let it happen?*

Morgan, who stood behind Katie, reached his arms over her shoulders. He pulled her close to him, folding his arms under her neck. "Sorry," he whispered. "I just couldn't help it. You looked like you were cold. And I . . . well, I just couldn't help it."

How strange. I feel like I could cry. Being next to Morgan with his arms around her was like coming home—to her real home. It felt almost like it was what she had been waiting for her whole life.

"Of course," added Morgan, somewhat loosening his hold on her, "if I'm being annoying . . . ."

"No, no," Katie answered quickly. "I was cold." And she found herself leaning her head back against his shoulder.

At the next station, as she stood with Morgan, Katie listened to the story of George Padley and Sarah Franks. Sarah and George, who were engaged to be married even before they started the trek. George and Sarah, who loved each other so much and had so much faith that they couldn't imagine being married anywhere else except in Zion, there to be married in the temple of God for the eternities. Sarah, who wrapped the dead body of her beloved George in the beautiful shawl she had brought with her from her homeland. Sarah, who asked for help to hang George's body, wrapped in the shawl, from the high limb of a tree there in the ravine so that the wolves would not ravage it.

Katie looked at Morgan. She looked at the somber faces of Pa and Ma, Heather, Zach, Lindsay, and Micah. She imagined them all dying. And she was the only one of them left. And the wolves waited until dark.

Turning her face to the walls of the ravine, Katie noticed scores of swallow nests built upon a rocky overhang on the steep hillside, half spheres jammed side by side, even constructed on top of each other. The nests seemed like just empty shells; Katie saw no swallows. The nests would eventually disintegrate from the destruction of the elements and would fall away and be blown in the wind. But not the swallows. They would fly. From their nests they had long ago flown.

Katie awoke very early the next morning, before it was light. *Too early*, thought Katie, and turning over, she pulled her bag up over most of her face to shut out the chill and went back to sleep.

Then she had another dream. She walked with the men, women, and children of the Martin Handcart Company. The cold was bitter and biting; the snow blew at her incessantly. Katie was surprised that she felt no chill in her toes. She realized that they were frozen, along with her fingers. Her stomach was empty, but she had long ago ceased to feel hunger. She only felt weak. And her mind felt numb. If she could only stop to rest just for a moment. Up ahead she noticed that there lay again a river to be crossed. Those ahead of her were trudging through slowly, so slowly that it was almost as if they did not move at all. Then Katie was there at the bank of the river. She dropped down on her knees and cried. She could not cross. She would just rest there and die. Surely dying would be an easier and better thing.

Suddenly there appeared by her side a beautiful woman with long, flowing, dark hair. The woman radiated faith, goodwill, and serenity. She stood dressed like a pioneer, but her dress and bonnet hung perfectly, without blemish. The woman was obviously not a member of their handcart company. Perhaps she was an angel.

"You will be all right," said the woman to Katie, in the most beautiful voice Katie had ever heard. "We will cross together."

The woman lifted Katie in her arms, and Katie felt lighter than a cloud, as light and as warm as rays of sunshine on a summer day. In her hand, the woman somehow held an umbrella as well. And the umbrella sheltered them both from the snow as the woman waded calmly and with great strength, with Katie in her arms.

Then Katie awoke.

Seventeen

Lying flat against the buffalo grass, her dark neck stretched out unnaturally, her nose pressed close to the ground, Josephine appeared not only unwilling, but this time also unable to move. Isaac patted the horse's neck with his hand.

"C'mon, Josephine, you just have to get up," he said. "Alfred can't pull the wagon without you. Josephine, please get up!"

Turning her right eye toward Isaac, Josephine looked at him for a few seconds as if she were considering his request and then shut her eye again and nuzzled further into the grass as if to say, "Sorry, boy. Go away and let me die in peace." Josephine had shown little interest in eating for the past several days; this morning she had refused to drink as well.

"Let's be allowin' the animal rest, now, me boy," advised Maddie, taking Isaac's hand to pull him up. "'Sure herself's entirely exhausted; perhaps given a little rest she'll come 'round."

Katherine stood up as well. "Yes, Isaac. Let's leave her alone for a while. Maybe she'd rather eat without us watching her."

Walking off to the side a little with Madeline, Katherine spoke quietly so that Isaac would not hear. "Nathanial knows a lot about horses, Maddie. But he must be far up the trail right now. He told me last night that there was to be a meeting of group captains this morning."

"Aye, your man has an altogether grand way with the animals, he does. And a way with you now, m'lady, I've been noticin'—if I may say so," added Maddie, her mouth twisting up to the side and her eyes narrowing into an I-wasn't-born-yesterday look.

Katherine chuckled. "Yes, you may say so, Maddie. I must confess. I love him! I love him. I truly, truly do! And now you know. And yes, I am now potted in the right pot, and it is all because of you." She laughed.

"Well, and to be sure I'm not wantin' to take for meself all the glory, now." Maddie smiled. "But a wee bit won't split the potatoes, now, will it?"

"No, a wee bit will not indeed be splittin' the potatoes," Katherine said as she imitated Maddie's accent.

"And now that that be settled, Katie, what should we do about the horses? The train will be pullin' out in an hour or so, I do believe."

"An idea occurred to me. Alfred has never been able to pull the wagon by himself, but perhaps he could if we lightened the wagon by taking out the trunk. The two of us could not lift the trunk out by ourselves, though. We would have to wait until Nathanial gets back—or ask Sam to help us."

"Even then, though, Katie, dear. We can't be certain that old Alfred will have the strength to pull the wagon, now can we?"

"No, Maddie. We can't," she responded. Katherine pushed loose strands of dusty hair back inside her faded bonnet and looked up at the high ravines and tips of the mountains.

"Are you after believin' the answer is up there, then?" asked Maddie.

"When God visits the earth, Maddie, I think that is where He goes. Where else would He be? I think He walks in the forests up there sometimes. Maybe He's there now. And maybe He's watching us. I think He knows we need the wagon."

The team of horses, along with the wagon, food, and other supplies for the journey, were all that Katherine owned, their homestead in Nauvoo having been left to the invaders. With the constant threat of mob attack and the subsequent call from Brigham Young to go West, Michael had fortunately insisted they ready themselves early for the journey. Grandmother Devonshire had passed away the preceding winter and left exactly $5000 to Katherine. With that money, and not a penny to spare, Michael purchased a wagon, Alfred and Josephine, 800 pounds of flour, 80 pounds of sugar, farming tools, seeds, and all else they would need for the trek and their settling into the Salt Lake Valley.

Isaac neared. "Are you done with your secret talk, mother?" he asked, just a tiny bit cocky.

"Yes, Isaac, we are done. And you," she added, kneeling down to hug him, "are a know-it-all!"

Isaac giggled a little. "But what about Josephine? How are we going to get her to eat?"

"See the sun coming up over that hill, Isaac?" asked his mother in reply.

"I see it," he replied in a whatever-can-this-have-to-do-with-Josephine tone of voice.

"And do you see it coming up every morning?"

"Yes, of course I do."

"Well, God is like that, and so is faith."

Isaac waited for his mother's explanation for quite a few seconds, but since she obviously was not planning to explain herself until he asked, he did so. "Okay, tell me. How are God and faith like the sun?" he finally asked.

"I'd like to hear this too, Katie, dear," added Maddie, stretching her cloak around to cover her broad shoulders. "Go on, then, and preach to us both."

Picking Isaac up in her arms, Katherine tilted his chin to the sun. "Do you feel the sunshine? God's love for us is always there, just like the warmth of the sun. Sometimes, it's a cloudy day or the earth has turned and taken us away from the sun's light. But His love is always there, and eventually it will shine on us.

"But you see, our faith needs to be like the sun too—it needs to come up every morning, no matter what difficulties we come across. Josephine is sick. She may live or she may die, but somehow our Father in Heaven will provide for us. He will make it possible in one way or another for us to do what He has asked of us, which in this case is to cross these plains and mountains."

"Do you believe that, Isaac?" asked his mother when she had finished.

"If you believe it, then I believe it," Isaac replied firmly.

"Well, then," said Maddie. "For sure 'tis so. Me mother was wont to say that without faith a man might as well give up the ghost now and be done with it. She said that and she meant it, she did. She was a good woman, as good as and better than most you'd find, 'tis true. Well," added Maddie, catching a deep breath, "it would be time now for breakfast."

"Just one second," said Isaac. Running to the wagon to fetch his blanket, he stretched it over Josephine to keep her from the morning chill.

In the distance Katherine and Maddie had earlier noticed a small group of buffalo lying in a circular formation on the ground, dark humps protruding from the green of the grass, lighter-colored calves peppering the circle. Now, as Katherine put away the tin cups and plates after breakfast, the buffalo suddenly lurched up and bolted to the north, the calves scrambling to their feet to scamper after their mothers. To the west of the herd, smoke arose on the horizon.

"It's a grass fire!" Sam yelled out, running from wagon to wagon. "We have to move out—now!"

Katherine ran to Josephine. Lifting the horse's head up from the ground a few inches, Katherine looked into her open eyes and spoke with authority and urgency. "Josephine, we have no time. We have no time to get the trunk out and see if Alfred can pull the wagon. We have no more time for you to rest and no more time for you to be sick. We have no time for you to die, Josephine."

Katherine dragged the water pan over to the horse's mouth. "Please, drink the water. Drink it now, Josephine!"

The horse snorted. Perhaps she smelled the smoke. Sliding her nose to the pan, Josephine began licking and then sucking the water. Katherine held grass to the horse's mouth, and, at first licking at it as she had the water, Josephine then took a mouthful and began to move it around slowly in her mouth.

With great effort, still snorting at the smoke in the air, Josephine swung her head around and tried to put weight on her forelegs. Her legs shook, though, and she dropped back to the ground.

"Come on, girl! You can do it!" encouraged Katherine as Maddie, hurriedly packing up the camp with Isaac, looked on from a distance.

Josephine tried again. Snorting once more, she threw her whole body into the effort, her legs flailing in every direction. Her feet somehow caught hold, though, and her muscles remained steadfast. Josephine's legs heaved all of the one thousand plus pounds of her upright.

Greatly relieved, Katherine held grass and water to the horse's mouth as she led her carefully, but as quickly as possible, to her position at the front of the wagon.

"She's not feeling well, Alfred," Katherine whispered to the other horse as she gently patted both of them. "So go slow and carry more than your share for a while."

"Let's walk, Maddie," Katherine said. "It will lighten Josephine's load."

As Katherine took Isaac's hand in hers, Maddie reached for the reins, clicked her tongue, and flicked the reins lightly. "Off wi'ya now!" she called out loudly to Alfred and Josephine. And the horses walked along. Both of them.

"Did God just shine on us, mother?" asked Isaac, looking up at her.

"Yes, Isaac, I believe He did." She smiled.

As the wagon train veered to the south of the burning grass, ashes began falling from the sky, at first lightly, like a dusting of powdered sugar on a pancake, and then more heavily, until little of the canvas remained visible on the covers of the wagons. The travelers looked like chimney sweeps, ash-covered except for the whites of their eyes.

"Look there, Maddie," called out Katherine as she pointed to a hill north of the fire. Mounted on six white horses that, despite the roaring conflagration below them, stood solid and unflinching, six Indians stared in their direction. Their message was clear. This is our land.

"Can you believe those horses, Maddie?" asked Katherine. "Most animals would be crazed with fear of the fire. They don't even move!"

"A testimony to the fact, dearie, that this is by far not the first occasion at which those horses ha' been present when a brush fire was lit."

Katherine had heard that at times the Indians burned the prairie grass to force the buffalo to move on to other pastures where the wagoneers could not hunt them.

What would it be like to be one of them? One with the land and the sky. Then we come. We threaten their source of survival, threaten their land and their lives. What would it be like to carry my baby tied onto my back? To raise my child in a tent?

"Look, Mother! Their spears are raised!"

Katherine looked up. The spears indeed appeared very threatening. "Quick!" ordered Katherine. "Jump in the wagon!"

Isaac scrambled into the back while Maddie stopped the horses so that she and Katherine could climb up.

The wagon train did not stop and circle, however, as it often did when there was an Indian scare, but continued pushing on cautiously to the southwest. As the spears of the Indians remained raised to the sky, the feathers attached to their spears fluttered in the breeze, and the fire below the Indians burned on, hot and bright.

Galloping his horse hard and fast toward them, Nathanial

reined in at Katherine's wagon. "Are you all right?" he asked, out of breath. "I came as fast as I could. Two wagons at the front of the wagon train caught fire."

"We're fine," answered Katherine. "Was anyone hurt?"

"No. No one. But we couldn't get the fire out in time to save one of the wagons," added Nathanial.

"I don't know how they'll get along without their wagon," responded Katherine. "Thank heavens, though, that no one was hurt. We almost lost our wagon too. I have a story to tell you about Josephine."

As Katherine and Nathanial talked and the wagon moved on, the smoke soon blinded their view of the Indians until they became a distant, silent threat behind them.

⁂

After a while, Katherine realized she was exhausted, probably from the morning's ordeal. Excusing herself, she climbed into an empty corner in the bed of the wagon and relaxed into its creaking and swaying.

"Gosh, Nathanial, those Indians looked like they wanted to kill us all!" was the last Katherine heard of the continuing conversation before sleep overtook her.

She dreamt she stood on the east bank of the Mississippi river, near Nauvoo. Along the river, small clusters of people, shoddily dressed, huddled together in an attempt to shut out the cold. The snow fell fast and thick, and a strong wind blew it into flurries. Though the river floated ice, some waded through. There was an urgency to cross. Katherine understood hunger in the sunken cheeks and loose skin of the faces of those who remained on the bank, exhaustion in the slow and unsteady movements of their hands, and she read death in their eyes. Most of them, Katherine knew, would not attempt to cross the river. They would die on the bank.

Though the scene was of the worst freezing conditions Katherine had ever witnessed, she was surprised to feel little cold. She wondered also at the umbrella at her side. Without doubt, however, she knew there was someone she must find, someone she must help. The need to find her was almost overwhelming. Though she searched the bank and the river, Katherine saw no one she recognized.

Lifting her eyes to the opposite bank, Katherine saw her own dear mother. She was beautifully dressed in an embroidered white robe, and she smiled at Katherine.

"Look," her mother said. Katherine's grandmother stood by Katherine's mother. She smiled at Katherine as well. Many others whom Katherine did not recognize stood behind them, a long line of Katherine's ancestors that reached into the thicket of trees and back into the hills.

Katherine's mother smiled and gestured for Katherine to look behind her. Turning around, Katherine saw Isaac, but grown into a man. Several stood behind him. They were her descendants, Katherine knew.

The last of them she recognized. It was the girl for whom Katherine had been searching, the face she had seen reflected in the water. The girl, really a young woman, sat hunched on the ground. She looked up at Katherine. Beautiful, with long dark hair like Katherine's own, but with pain-filled eyes, the girl had to cross the river in order to survive. Katherine knew she must take her. She belonged to Katherine and to Isaac and to Isaac's son and to his son. She belonged to Katherine's mother. She belonged to them all.

"Come, Katherine," she said to the young lady, somehow knowing her name was the same as her own. "We will cross the river together."

Katherine opened her umbrella, and immediately it warmed both her and the girl and gave Katherine strength. Taking the young woman up into her arms, she waded without effort across the icy river.

Then the wagon jarred as a front wheel rolled over a large rock, and Katherine awoke.

The lowering afternoon sun still burned hot and bright as Katherine's company circled to camp at the base of Independence Rock. It was July 18, two weeks after the recommended time to pass the well-known landmark. Katherine hoped that their lateness would not signify crossing the Rocky Mountains in heavy snow. Severe winter storms could cause delays, and their supplies of food and clothing were already being used up much faster than expected.

At least the size of a small hill, Independence Rock was huge but seemed to be made up of just that—one rock. Sam and Sarah, with baby Jacob wrapped tightly at her chest, walked with Maddie and Isaac toward the rock. Nathanial and Katherine followed close behind them, his arm wrapped loosely around her shoulder. The two often laughed and turned to look at each other. Phoebe and Marsha talked a short way behind them, but Katherine and Nathanial pretended not to hear.

"Michael must be rolling over in his grave right now," complained Marsha in a voice obviously meant to be heard by more than just her friend.

"Such a fine man Michael was too," agreed Phoebe. "And to think she would trade him for—" she cupped her hand to the side of her mouth and leaned her head toward Marsha's "—for a ruffian!"

"It hasn't even been a year, you know," added Marsha. Afraid though that she had not spoken loud enough, she said it again. "Do you realize, Phoebe, dear, that it hasn't even been one year since—" Here, though, Marsha tripped and squealed as she went down. She hadn't been paying attention to the pathway and had slipped on a small rock.

Hurrying to Marsha's aid, Nathanial took her arm and helped her to stand. It wasn't easy. Marsha was extremely heavy.

"Are you all right, Sister Marsha?" Nathanial asked, careful to hide his amusement.

"I believe so, Brother," she replied. Brushing the dirt off her skirt, she added, "I do thank you for your kindness."

"Anytime, Sister Marsha. Anytime I can be of assistance to you in any way, just ask me." Nathanial tipped his hat to her and joined Katherine, who smiled at Marsha and Phoebe from up the trail.

As the group neared the rock, they saw many names etched and painted on its face and more than a few members of the wagon train now leaving their own names.

"I heard that Jim Bridger carved his name here," commented Sarah, placing her hand at her brow to shut out the glare of the sun while her eyes scanned some of the names on the rock.

Isaac's face suddenly gleamed with excitement. "I'll bet I can find it!" he exclaimed. "May I go look, Mama? May I?"

Katherine glanced up high to the top of the rock. It looked steep—and slick, too. "I don't know, Isaac. It looks dangerous."

"I'll take him up, Katherine," offered Nathanial. "Maybe we can spot a horned Hercules beetle while we're up there," he added with a wink at Isaac.

"Wow! Can we, Mama?"

"All right, then. But be careful, Isaac, and stay with Nathanial."

"I will, Mama!" He sprinted off, kicking up dust as he ran. Nathanial followed behind him and then turned to wave and smile at Katherine.

Incredible! His smile is just like my father's! And I never noticed it before!

From the base of the rock, a man called out to Katherine, Maddie, Sarah, and Sam. Seated atop a small boulder, his grayed clothing, smoky hair, and lined face blending in with the colors and textures that surrounded him, the man seemed a part of the landmark.

"How about placing your names on the rock for posterity?" asked the man. "Three dollars buys your name engraved with today's date. I'm a stonecutter. The job I do is professional, and it's guaranteed to last. What do you say?" he asked, spitting in the dirt to the side of him.

Puzzled, Katherine asked, "Are you from our wagon train?"

"No, ma'am," answered the man, a quick clip to his voice. "That over there's my train—and he waved his faded and dusty hat toward an old tent a number of feet from the rock. The darkened ring of a fire pit, numerous discarded tin cans and cooking equipment were strewn about near it as evidence of his claim to the campground and its longevity.

"Sorry," answered Sam for them all. "No money."

Smiling and walking on, Katherine heard the man soon calling the same question to other passersby. For posterity . . . For posterity! Suddenly she wished more than anything that she had three dollars.

There must be a way. "Sarah, Sam, Maddie—I'll see you later. I'm going to climb up," Katherine told her friends as she quickened her steps to almost a run.

"Wait, we'll come with you," called Sarah.

Katherine turned. "No. No . . . I'll see you soon. I need to be by myself for a while." And she was off before Sarah could say anything else.

Looking for a place to ascend, Katherine began circling the rock. Tall, marshy plants grew thickly around the back side that, along with hordes of mosquitoes, made it difficult to approach. As she turned a corner, she was startled by a near miss with a large, ugly, orange- and black-ringed lizard. Her boot could have smashed it flat, but fortunately she felt the lizard underfoot in time and escaped having to scrape its innards from the bottom of her shoe.

Finally, after circling halfway around, Katherine found a spot where she was able to get a good foothold and pull herself up to a slight overhang. It was easy, then, to walk up the rock to its highest point.

The rock was even higher than Katherine expected. Down below, the people and wagons looked like little miniatures, much like an expensive set of toy soldiers and battlements Katherine had seen in a drugstore window. But what a view! To the west, she recognized Devil's Gate; Katherine had seen drawings of it while preparing at Winter Quarters to continue west. To the north of Devil's Gate, a small lake glinted back the sun as did the waters of the Sweetwater, which flowed near the rock and wound around the foot of the mountains to the southwest.

A scripture played out in Katherine's mind. It was Lehi pleading with his son. "O that thou mightest be like unto this river, continually running into the fountain of all righteousness!"

Is that what I should write on the rock? Sometimes scriptures ran through her mind, and often she found them to be a resolution to something that had been troubling her or an answer to a prayer. What message could Katherine possibly leave for her descendant that would make a difference in her life?

A warm wind blew back Katherine's hair and bonnet, and she hoped Isaac and Nathanial were holding fast to the rock somewhere on the other side. *Hmmm . . . Hold fast to the rock.*

Well, it will come to me. She began examining the names on the rock. Those which were shallowly engraved—even those that dated only a year or two earlier—were difficult to decipher, while the names obviously engraved with tools looked as permanent as a gravestone professionally made to order. Some names were written in ordinary paint, but those names were fading quickly as well.

Katherine searched in her mind for something in her wagon that she could sell for three dollars and do without, but she could think of nothing. All of their clothing and bedding they would need in the colder part of their journey, and Katherine doubted the man would want any of them. Their food and equipment they could not do without.

Glancing around at the names again, Katherine noticed one painted in black that stood out markedly from the rest. CJ MILLET ILL 1844. As she neared and bent to examine the writing, she realized that it was written with tar, not paint. Not only was the writing unfaded, but the tar still stood out from the rock face. It looked as if it would last forever.

As Katherine walked on, she found that though she saw

fifteen or twenty people writing on the rock, none were using tar. While some etched with sharp rocks or knives, others drew with a thick white paint. Katherine hadn't a clue as to who, if anyone, in the wagon train might have tar.

She turned back the way she had come to climb down the rock. It wouldn't do any good to write a message that wouldn't last. Perhaps Katherine could find something in her wagon, after all, that she could bargain with. Climbing up the rock, though, had been much easier than climbing down. After reaching the overhang, she tried climbing down facing the rock and then with her back to it, but each seemed equally impossible. Just as she was about to give up and find an easier spot to descend, though, Katherine noticed a spring of water in a crevice of the rock just to the left below her. Since it sprang from a side hidden to her view from the way she had come, she had not noticed it earlier.

Realizing that she was very thirsty, she decided to take her chances. Turning to face the rock, which felt somewhat safer, she very slowly lowered herself handhold by foothold, keeping her weight to the rock as well as she could. With five or six feet left to descend, however, her foot slipped, and Katherine's hands scraped over the rock as she tried to find something to grab onto while she slid. She could catch hold of nothing, though, and, landing rear-first in a cluster of reeds, she fell backward into a swampy muck.

Well, at least no broken bones. Katherine stood and examined her hurting hands. They were scraped badly and, in fact, bleeding in several places. As she pushed her way through the reeds with the back of her hands, she noticed a bucket to the right of her nestled in the reeds. The bucket—almost empty—still contained an inch or two of wet tar. Someone had obviously left it there quite recently.

Having long ago ceased to doubt miracles, Katherine felt sure the bucket was meant for her. After all, if the Lord could inspire her heart and thoughts to turn to her descendant, surely He could inspire someone to leave right here and now this bucket of leftover tar. Gently lifting the bucket by its handle with just the ends of her fingertips, Katherine carried it out of the reeds and set it down near the crevice where she had seen the trickle of water.

She looked up. Sure enough, the water ran there, hidden at the very back of a large crevice. She could see it just at its highest point. The sun blaring hot and high, the water looked better than ever. Katherine squeezed through a narrow passageway in the rock and made her way through a small opening. At full view now, the spring of water ran down the face of the rock into what appeared to be another spring below on the ground. There, at its deepest point, the water bubbled.

Bending down, Katherine washed her hands in a shallow section, rubbing the dirt off the onyx ring her father had given her before she left Nauvoo. Once her hands were clean, she cupped them into the water at its deepest, clearest point and drank fully. It was the most delicious water Katherine had ever tasted. Then tearing off two sections of her petticoat, she wrapped her hands and tucked the ends of the bandages under. That seemed to stop the bleeding.

The hidden crevice is the perfect place to write, she thought. Free from the erosion of wind and protected to a great extent from the rain, the writing would last much longer there. True, the spot would not be plainly visible nor easy to find, but Katherine was sure that her descendant would be led to it. This was the writing that would make the connection. This was the answer. She was sure.

Carrying the bucket inside the crevice, Katherine stirred the tar with her wrapped hand and lifted it to write on the wall opposite the spring. My descendant must know that this miracle is for her, the miracle that I should be given to know her name, that I should be drawn to her. That, above all, the Lord remembers her—specifically and most surely—right now. And that He is reaching down to lift her close to Him.

Taking a big breath and pondering before each word, Katherine wrote. And she was satisfied.

Eighteen

With eyes wide open and fingers laced together behind her head, Katie lay in her tent and thought. She knew it was time to get up. Heather and Micah had dressed and left the tent long ago while Katie had pretended to be asleep. A bugle sounded in the distance. The morning devotional must be just starting. As they did each morning, everyone else would be circled around a flag mounted at the corner of a cart, listening to the morning prayer, the men holding their cowboy hats in their hands. You could almost feel the quiet at those times, and Katie imagined it was so now.

Katie knew quiet. A different kind of quiet, though. The quiet of her mother's sadness. The quiet after her mother passed out at night, having drunk way too much. The quiet of the house in the morning as Katie got ready for school and her mother lay in bed, dead to the world. Last of all—or more precisely, first of all—the quiet after the storm of words before her father slammed the door and never came back. That first quiet, which caused all the rest.

The silence of the morning devotional prayer was much different though. Instead of bringing isolation, that quiet united all who stood in the circle. Katie felt as if they all shared one voice, articulated by the person who offered the prayer. Instead of despair, the quiet of the prayer became hope itself. Still Katie felt unsure. She didn't know if she could really be like all of them.

At the same time, she was afraid to be separated from them, afraid she would lose the peace they had given her and even lose the wanting to be like them. Morgan, especially, seemed to see something good in Katie that she was just beginning to see herself. And sometimes when she looked at Morgan, it was like looking at someone she had always known—someone she always wanted to be with.

Today was the last day of the trek, though. A caravan of vehicles would be arriving tomorrow at sunup to shuttle them all back. Of course, Morgan had planned to get together with Katie after the trek. But Katie didn't know how that could work out.

I can just imagine Morgan meeting my mother. He'll come to pick me up, and she'll be in her usual position—drunk on the couch, the TV blaring. He'll say, "Hi, Mrs. McBride. I'm Morgan. I'm glad to meet you."

And she'll reply, "Good to meet . . . good to . . . glad you could come. By the way," she'll add as she swings her bottle in a half circle up to her mouth and guzzles. "By the way, did Katie ever tell you about her little meth party and the night she spent at the police station? See this scar?" she'll ask, pointing to her arm. "Katie did that to me."

Katie was certain that would be the first and last time she would hang out with Morgan. *Oh, sure, he'll be polite. He'll still take me to ride Lady. But he'll never call me again.*

It was darker and more chilly in the tent than it had usually been at this time in the morning; Katie imagined it must be cloudy outside. Stretching her arms high to a dull, misty light emanating through the tent flap opening, she examined her hands. The same hands that had stolen an iPod from a locker just three weeks ago. Sure, Katie would make sure she got Laura Drummond's iPod back to her, but that didn't take away the fact that Katie had stolen it in the first place. Nor the fact that she had stolen things before. *Morgan wouldn't ever steal anything.* Katie was positive of that. *And neither would Heather, Micah, Zach, or Lindsay. Just me.*

Katie took a deep breath and let it out slowly as she remembered that she had also been totally unable to control her hands as they slammed into her mother, cutting her mother's arm and causing her nose to bleed. It seemed such a long time ago. Yes, Katie's mother had done the same to her before and much worse, and, yes, Katie had been very afraid of what her mother might do to her while drunk, but those were not sufficient excuses. There were no good excuses.

Katie's hands were large with long and narrow fingers. Her mother's were small; her fingers more than an inch shorter than Katie's. *My hands must be like my dad's. I'm like my dad.* Abruptly dropping her hands to her sides, Katie turned her eyes, smarting with tears, to the side of the tent. *I don't know if I can do it. Maybe I can't be a friend to God. Maybe the person I'm trying to be now is only fake. Maybe I'll wake up soon, and I'll just be the real me again. The me who can't seem to do anything right. Who fails. Who chooses to fail. The me who is like my dad. And my mother.*

Two boys began talking outside of the tent, perhaps about twenty feet away, stragglers to the devotional. "Wait up, dude!" called out one. "My shoes are untied!"

"Your shoes are always untied! Why do you have to tie them now?" the other responded.

"Because I want to be like you, of course," said the first sarcastically. "Just wait, okay?"

His voice. Katie had heard it before—lots of times. That's right! It was the voice that gave the announcements every Monday over the loudspeaker at school, the voice of Sean Adamson, the senior class president. Katie had had a crush on Sean many times; every new school year, after she had gone through a new guy she liked, she always came back to Sean. But from afar off—extremely far. Sean played on the school football team, he was smart, and he was "way hot."

"You know whose tent this is?" Sean asked, not expecting an answer. "It's Heather Garcia's and Micah Lancaster's."

"I don't know who Micah is," responded the other boy.

"Dude! You don't know who Micah is? You're kidding! Micah Lancaster is the hottest cheerleader. You have to know who she is! Long blonde hair . . . cute little freckles . . . she's gorgeous. She drives a blue mustang to school."

"O-o-o-h yeah. She's hooked up with Chris Anderson. Too bad she doesn't know she's one of his many."

"Right," said Sean. "Chris never sticks with one chick. But that just leaves me room to make my move." Then he dramatized a wild Dracula laugh—as if he had his sights on a particularly soft and delicious white neck.

"And you know who else is in her group?" Sean asked. "Katie McBride." And then he said "Psy-cho!" in a singsong voice. Katie just knew that at the same time he was twirling his finger in circles at his head.

"Always keep your distance from that girl," he continued. "Gustavo tells me she tried to murder her own mom, and it landed her in juvie. She's known as quite the little thief too."

"Well, she's on this trek, isn't she? That must mean something. Maybe she's changed."

"What a joke!" Sean said. "Katie McBride is doomed. Just wait. She's bound to be a junky, and nothin' could save her. She'll have tracks running up and down her arms. Guaranteed—she'll be in jail for most of her life."

"Sounds like your kind of chick," joked Sean's friend. "Don't worry, though, I'm sure the jail will have visiting hours."

Sean laughed as they walked away, a loud not-me-in-a-million-years laugh, a laugh that made Katie curl up inside. His laugh continued until the sound of their voices faded in the distance. Katie closed her eyes to shut out what she had just overheard. But the sound of Sean's laugh wouldn't die.

Eager now to leave her tent, Katie quickly pulled her dress over her undershirt and bloomers and brushed through her hair. She grabbed her water bottle, toothbrush, and toothpaste, zipped open the tent door, and walked out.

As she veered from the pathway to find a bush over which to brush her teeth, Katie came face to face with the strangest looking lizard she had ever seen, perched on a small boulder. Its neck was collared with two thick rings of black centered with a ring of bright orange, and the surrounding flesh appeared to be a yellowish mush. Orange stripes ran down the lizard's back and faded into its tail, the tail making up at least half of its total length. The lizard must have been more than a foot long.

Katie held completely still. For perhaps a full minute, the lizard stared at her with two deep black-bead eyes. Katie had a crazy, yet distinct, impression that the lizard was reading her mind, or at least trying to communicate with her somehow. It then startled her by dashing away at super-speed as if it were fleeing a horrific monster. Its fingers gripping rock to rock and its belly sailing high off the ground, it was like some fantastic computer-animated creature from *Star Wars*.

Katie had no idea that lizards had extrasensory perception, but she was sure this one did. How else would it have so inexplicably known what everyone else seemed to know: that at all costs Katie McBride should be avoided. She had tried to change before. A counselor at the school had talked her into it. At the time it had seemed like a good idea. She stopped going to late-night parties, never missed a day of school, and began doing her work in class; she even started carrying her books home to complete unfinished work and to study for tests. Her grades immediately shot up. On her next grade report, Katie amazed herself with almost straight A's.

She even decided to show her mother her grades. That was a mistake. Instead of being excited for her daughter and proud of her, Katie's mother showed no emotion.

"Your dad got good grades," her mother said finally. "It didn't do much for him."

After that Katie lost interest. She decided it was too much work, after all. It didn't seem worth all the trouble. Her counselor was disappointed, but—hey—it was Katie's life, not his.

I'm not a person who can change. I'm not like other people. Sean knows it. And my mom knows it. I'll bet my dad knew it, and I know it. And even some stupid lizard knows it.

Katie brushed her teeth and made plans. Big plans. *I don't belong here with these people. I'll walk. And I'll keep on walking. No one will even know I'm gone, not at least for a while, anyway. I don't belong here. I'm not like them. I can't be.*

Katie's thoughts turned to her ancestor Katherine. *It's too bad they gave me her name. I wonder if they meant to. If I try to be like her, or like the kids on this trek, I won't be able to. I'll be a disgrace to her name. It's too late for me to be different. I've gone too far. I've done too much. God doesn't want people like me on His side. I'm not good enough.*

Katie remembered the peas. A long time ago, before Katie's father left, her mother would plant a garden every spring. The peas were always to be planted first, as soon as the ground was safe from frost. Checking the garden each morning, Katie waited eagerly for the first flowers of the pea plants, the first emergence of tiny pods, and then the first pod that bulged. She loved to snap them open at the round, flat end and drop the sweet little peas in her mouth. Much too soon each year, though, the weather would become too hot for the delicate pea plants, and the vines would dry up and die.

One summer, the last summer of their garden, the pods hung unpicked on the plants, and, as the heat withered the rows of peas, the engorged pods dried and spilled wrinkled, tan-colored little balls on the garden floor. Katie picked a few up in her hand and then threw them back to the garden.

In mid-September, Katie walked into the garden and found three to four-inch pea plants growing sporadically where the dried peas had fallen. *Too bad,* she thought then. *They look so healthy, but they'll never have peas. It's too late in the season. There's not enough time left before it will begin to frost at night. They're growing so well, but they'll never have peas. It's just too late for them.*

And it's too late for me. I'm like those peas. I tried, but it was too late for me to start.

Morgan's dark, piercing eyes shot out at Katie. Every time she looked into his eyes, Katie had the distinct impression that she had seen those eyes before, as if she had known Morgan already. And Pa and Ma—all of her trek family. *I mean something to them. They care about me. I'm sure they do.*

Tears welled in Katie's eyes, though, as her next thought discounted everyone she had come to know on the trek: *They're just pretending. They want me to become part of their church. "Each member a missionary." It's part of their religion. Pa told me. They don't really care about me any more than Sean Adamson does.*

A cold wind picked up, and Katie looked at the sky. She opened her eyes wide in amazement to see a huge thundercloud, miles wide with tall billowing white columns stretching out from the dark base. Shaped like a gigantic porcupine, the cloud looked as if it were poised to stamp its huge foot down upon the earth. The higher white billows were deceptive, lifting attention from the dark turbulence below. Katie remembered seeing a giant cloud like this once on television. A long, winding tornado funnel spun out of it.

It doesn't matter. Katie headed for her tent, intending to gather her things together to take with her. She soon realized, however, that there was very little there that she wanted. What a shame she didn't have a T-shirt and a pair of jeans to change into. While strong winds slapped and shook the tent, whipping the window and door flaps sharply, Katie threw on her jacket. She stuffed her flashlight, hairbrush, toothpaste and toothbrush, and washcloth into her sleeping bag and then rolled it up tight.

As she glanced at Katherine's journal and the scriptures that lay stacked at the side of her bucket, her heart ached a little. *I won't need them now. They'll just be in the way.* Still she picked up the two and ran her finger along Katherine's name on the journal. *I'll never read either one again.* Quickly setting them in her bucket, Katie grasped the rope that tied her sleeping bag and left the tent.

Immediately the wind whipped her pioneer skirt and tore her bonnet from her neck. Katie zipped her jacket to shut out the cold and then looked over at Independence Rock. It was immense. More like a tiny mountain than a rock. If she could make it to the south side without anyone seeing her, she could make a beeline from there to the highway. The rock would form a barrier between Katie and the handcart families, who now sat *en masse*, still at the devotional.

Cars drive by once in a while. I'll hitch a ride if I can. I'll find people like me. If not, I'll walk. Whatever happens, it doesn't matter. It's all the same. If they realize I'm gone, they won't search for long. No one will really care.

Moving quickly and purposefully, darting almost at a run around and over wet cow pies, Katie soon took cover behind the mountainous rock. Immediately she noticed name after name carved into or painted on the rock. S. A. Scott 1860. W. Haydock McBlean May 22, 1858. Last night Ma had told their group that thousands of names were left there on the rock, either carved with wagon repairing tools or painted with ordinary paint, wagon tar, or a mixture of black powder, buffalo grease, and glue. Ma seemed to know just about everything.

Pulling her windblown hair away from her eyes, Katie looked out at the highway. Since there were no cars in sight, she turned back to the names. Many of them were so faded or eroded that they were impossible to make out. Was it H. L. Chapin or H. L. Chapit? T. Swartwout or Swartwort? Katie was glad she didn't have a name like that. *Actually Swartwort is probably a much better name than McBride.* Katie imagined a knight by the name of Swartwort from Swartwort castle. He rode a magnificent white steed and brandished a great, ornate sword that almost burst with reflections of sunlight. Then she imagined a peasant digging potatoes from a garden outside the castle wall.

"McBride!" called the knight to the peasant. "Make sure you place every potato in the baskets today. You are fortunate that yesterday your hands weren't cut off for the potatoes you pocketed! On with it, then!" And Swartwort reared his white horse and galloped off. Probably to war or to save a princess in distress. *No, a million times better to be a Swartwort than a McBride.*

Now and again a lone, heavy drop of rain fell upon Katie. She glanced again at the highway and at the sky. Darkening the earth beneath even more, the clouds had lowered until black shrouds dropped to meet the surrounding mountaintops. It was difficult for Katie to see into the distance, especially with the wind lashing at her eyes. Still she was sure there were two or three cars a mile or so away, traveling toward her.

Gulping to swallow her fear, Katie picked up her sleeping bag, slipped the hood of her jacket over her head, and stepped away from Independence Rock. Bolts of lightning that had before been indistinct white flashes now turned into jagged, angry bars of fire. Then the rain fell. Hard. Turning back to the rock for cover, Katie noticed a cleft and ran toward it, water already dripping from her hair. She squeezed in through a narrow passage.

There Katie waited for what seemed an hour as tiny rivulets that had begun by crisscrossing the earth formed rapidly into muddy streams and deep puddles. Laying her head back against the rock, Katie closed her eyes. *I am so tired.* For several minutes she stood resting there without movement, water running over her closed eyelids, dripping off her still fingertips and face. *Oh, my sleeping bag must be drenched!*

Katie opened her eyes and noticed a white flower growing in a rocky crack at the base of the cleft. It appeared to be ... yes, it was! The same kind of flower Katherine had loved and drawn in her journal—a Sego Lily! As the rain slowed, Katie bent down to touch the flower. Three, triangular, large white petals vaguely streaked with purple floated atop a seven- or eight-inch, grasslike stem. Katie began digging with her fingers into the soft, black soil at its base. There, after digging about two inches, she found the bulb. The tiny bulb Katherine had described. It had to be the same flower.

Her digging having loosened the ground at the base of the rock, Katie now noticed some partially uncovered writing on the rock wall. Finding a flat rock, she worked for several minutes digging the earth away, and then she cleaned the dirt from the writing with the palm of her hand using the rainwater that dripped from the rock. The words were drawn in black; Katie guessed they were written with tar.

To Katherine McBride
Look
The Lord is with you
He is your strength
Katherine McBride 1848

Katie blinked her eyes hard and then opened them wide in amazement. *It's me! I'm the one she couldn't stop thinking of. Her journal was written to me! How did she know my name was the same as hers?*

Katie felt all the strength go out of her. Since it seemed her legs would hold her no longer, she scrunched down into the rock cleft and sat on the dirt floor. Her head swirled and seemed to float, as if it would sway her away, up and over the cleft. The storm had ceased, but Katie felt rain running down her cheeks. Sliding her fingertip across her jawline, she started to laugh. *Tears, not rain!*

What does all this mean? Her mind scrambled to pull the pieces together. *Why me? Why was Katherine inspired to think of me?* She lifted her eyes to heaven. Dark clouds still veiled most of the sky, but they split open directly east to allow the passage of a brilliant, elongated ray of sunlight. What Katie next felt she would remember for the rest of her life: it was as if that ray of sunlight poured directly into her deepest self, carrying with it an unbelievably expansive love—the love of God. Katie felt what she knew could never come from anything or anyone on earth. It filled her with an indescribable joy, and she wondered in amazement at the goodness of God.

Me? Why would God pour His love into me? But no sooner had she begun to think the thought than it melted away into a smile.

You are mine. The words flowed simply into Katie's mind. *You are mine. And I will lead you by the hand and give you strength.*

The sensations left her, but the words in Katie's thoughts circled unceasingly. *You are mine. I will lead you by the hand. I will give you strength.* Raindrops or teardrops still ran down Katie's face. It didn't matter to Katie which they were.

She slid her fingertips along the inscription and imagined Katherine there with her, both together in time, her pioneer ancestor drawing the words with a stick dipped in tar while she, Katie, traced the words with her fingers. Katie placed the palm of first one hand and then the other flat against the inscription on the rock. Gazing at her hands, she felt more than thought: *Our hands meet here.*

"Katie!" It was someone calling her name. Were they calling for her, though, or for her ancestor? Just for a split second, the years in Katie's mind blended into one. And then somehow she knew that not only was Katherine's name hers. Katherine's courage and strength were hers too. Perhaps they always had been.

"Katie!" exclaimed Pa, now standing over her with Morgan and Ma behind him. "We've been searching everywhere for you. Are you all right?" he asked as he bent to wipe the tears from her face.

She looked up into the concerned countenances of Pa, Ma, and Morgan.

Am I all right? Katie thought of her ancestor's journal—written to her—back in the tent and then of her own name painted on the rock. It was all a miracle. A miraculous gift of love from God to her. To her. Katherine May McBride.

How could she explain all that? The tale resonant in the depth and clarity of her black, Irish eyes, Katie simply smiled and extended her hand for a lift up.

Nineteen

Katie smiled and waited in her sleep for the next tap-tap-tap-tapping. Hail fell in patterned beats against the tent, almost like music—like handbells at Christmas. Soon she knew there would be wind whipping the tarp and rain pounding all around.

"Katie, Katie, wake up!" she heard. It was Micah's voice.

Katie squeezed her eyes tighter and rolled away from the sound. "Mmmm," she moaned. "Not yet . . . not yet. Let me sleep just a few more minutes." She pulled her crocheted bed-cover up over her eyes.

The tapping came again—not on the tent, though, but at the window! "C'mon, Katie, wake up! Come on out. We made breakfast!"

This time Katie sat up and rubbed her eyes. She was at home now, not on the trek. And there outside, almost pressed against the window, were the happy faces of Micah, Lindsay, and Heather. Her own face lit up, meeting the light coming through her window.

"Surprise!" All three called at the same time.

"Come outside! We have breakfast all set up on the grass in front," said Heather excitedly.

"Give me a minute!" Katie responded with the same excitement. "I'll be right out."

Quickly changing into the jeans and T-shirt she had left at the foot of her bed, Katie tiptoed past her mother's room, hurried to the bathroom, and gathered her hair into a ponytail.

She was about to open the door and walk out when she looked through the glass and saw Morgan and Zach with the three girls. Standing tall in a tan cowboy hat, Morgan looked just like a movie star playing the sheriff in a Western.

Katie ran back in to brush her teeth.

When she walked outside, they were all seated on a king-size bright-blue blanket that covered at least half of Katie's tiny lawn. She stopped to fully appreciate the picture. Katie felt a simple, pleasant sense of peace, recognized it, and smiled.

She offered the blessing on the breakfast. "We thank you, Heavenly Father, for this food. Please bless it. But thank you, Father, even more for giving us each other. And for your love. And help us not to wake up my mother. Amen."

When Katie opened her eyes, she saw a police car driving slowly by. The officer in the car held up his hand to say hello to Katie—it was the policeman who brought Katie home. Though it seemed like a year ago, she knew only a couple of months had gone by. Katie smiled at him and waved.

"Do you know him?" asked Micah.

"Yes. He's a friend." Then looking around, Katie laughed to herself and wondered at the sudden increase in her tally of friends.

"Okay! Let's eat!" exclaimed Morgan. "I don't know about you guys, but I'm starving." He lifted a huge, sticky cinnamon roll from a large plate and bit into it.

"None of you will believe this, but I got up at five o'clock this morning to make those rolls," Lindsay said as pancakes and syrup passed from hand to hand. "It's my mother's secret recipe. She actually won second place with them this summer in the city baking contest. So you better eat them all up!" She laughed. They could all tell, though, that she was serious.

"Don't worry," said Morgan. "I'll eat what everyone else doesn't." At least, Katie assumed that was what he said; she could hardly make out the words because his mouth was stuffed full.

"More syrup, Zach?" Micah laughed as he emptied the syrup bottle onto his plate. "You can't be serious. Are you having syrup with your pancakes or pancakes with your syrup?"

"You're absolutely right. Why pretend? Hey, Morgan, throw me that Butter Recipe Aunt Jemima, will you?"

Catching the bottle easily, Zach popped open the top and began chugging down the syrup as if it were a bottle of root beer. "Now that's more like it!" he exclaimed.

"Oo—ooh, yuck!" squealed Micah. "That is so disgusting!"

Katie glanced up at her mother's window. "Micah," she cautioned. "We have to keep our voices down. We'll wake up my mom."

"Oh, sorry," Micah quickly replied. "I forgot."

"Maybe you'd like to try that with the butter, Zach," said Morgan, almost whispering. "Bet you can't eat the whole cube!"

Before Zach could answer, though, the screen door of the porch creaked open on its hinges, bringing Katie's mother with it.

"What's going on?" she questioned in a dragging voice. "What's all this racket?" The silky black top and loose-fitting jeans she wore hung wrinkled and twisted while her hair fell fuzzy and bent. Her mouth drooped too, slack and sort of crooked, but still accusing.

Katie looked at Morgan first, but she saw no reaction in his face. His body seemed frozen in place, though. And so were the bodies of Lindsay, Zach, Heather, and Micah. Their eyes were also frozen, frozen wide and full of an emotion Katie couldn't quite identify—perhaps a mix of shock and fear.

"Katie!" demanded her mother when no one spoke. "I asked you what's going on!" She stepped out from the doorway, letting the screen door shut with a bang behind her.

Morgan stood up. "Mrs. McBride, we are so sorry we woke you up. We really were trying to be quiet. We're having a little breakfast picnic. It was a surprise. Katie had no idea. We brought tons of food. Would you like some pancakes—or maybe some strawberries?" he asked, though Katie knew a sudden snowstorm would be much more likely than her mother accepting the offer.

Katie's mother lifted her hand to her hair and straightened it somewhat. "I don't think so," she replied as she turned to go back in. "I'll speak with you later, young lady," Mrs. McBride added as she shot a severe look in her daughter's direction. It felt like the electric chair to Katie.

"Don't worry, Katie," reassured Morgan. "Lindsay, give me one of your cinnamon rolls," he directed. "Hurry."

"No, Morgan," said Katie, tears of embarrassment in her eyes. "Forget about it. She'll be all right."

"No, my dear," Morgan replied in a voice mimicking Cary Grant. Or was it Jimmy Stewart? "A gentleman knows his duty and meets it."

A picture flashed into Katie's mind of a knight on a white steed. He carried a great sword in his hand instead of a cinnamon roll. She remembered that his name was Swartwort.

"I'm going in," declared Morgan.

"Okay. But I'm coming with you," she responded.

Balancing his peace offering, Morgan knocked softly and the two of them walked into the house after hearing a barely perceptible "Come in." They immediately found Katie's mother sitting on the sofa, a remote in one hand and a cigarette in the other.

"I brought you a cinnamon roll," Morgan said. "They're really too good to pass up. They actually won second place in a baking contest—Lindsay's mom's secret recipe."

"No, thanks," Katie's mother replied emphatically. "I already said no, didn't I?"

Hearing the anger in Mrs. McBride's voice, Morgan and Katie stepped toward the window and gazed out silently. The houses in Katie's neighborhood were older, made of brown or gray brick and cement. They must have been beautiful when they were built in the early 1900s, but now most were in bad repair. Forgotten and unappreciated, brick corners crumbled away, and painted doors and window frames were left to splinter and fade. The house on the corner appeared almost haunted, with three broken windows partially covered by out-grown weeds. Embarrassed, Katie followed Morgan's gaze as he looked at their old, broken fence and then at the collapsed carport just visible through the window.

"Mrs. McBride," Morgan began slowly. "I see your carport is damaged. What happened?"

"Oh, that stupid, rickety thing?" she replied as she blew out another mouthful of smoke. "It was bound to fall down sooner or later."

"You know, I think I could fix it. I mean, we could fix it, my dad and I. We do stuff like that all the time."

"Sorry, kid," Katie's mother responded. "I'm fresh out of money." Katie's eyes grew wide at her mother's blunt remark, but she said nothing.

Morgan laughed—politely, though. "Oh, no. You wouldn't need to pay me. And, actually, I think we have some extra two-by-fours and some plywood in the barn. I'll bet we already have everything we need. So it wouldn't cost anything."

Mrs. McBride put out her cigarette in a pea-green ash-tray that looked like it had been saved from the sixties. For the first time, she looked Morgan directly in the face, and she seemed surprised—pleasantly surprised—but still skeptical. She remained silent for a moment.

"We don't need charity, though. Are you sure you won't be needin' that wood of yours?"

"No, ma'am. We won't need it. And I'll bet we can help you with your fence, too."

Katie's mother turned the TV off and straightened her position a little in the couch. "No one says ma'am anymore."

"I know, Mrs. McBride." Morgan laughed. "I can't help it, though. I belong to a long line of cowboys, and they've always said, 'ma'am.' I actually tried once to stop using it, but it felt weird, and I didn't know what to say instead."

"Well, I like it."

"Thank you, ma'am."

Katie's mother chuckled the tiniest of chuckles. "Tell me, then, young man. What's your name, and how do you know my Katie here?"

Twenty

"It's kind of squishy in here," Morgan said, his knees bent up high as he lay on the floor of the tree house. "Your dad must not have thought about you growing."

Katie lay next to him. "No. I don't think he did. I think he imagined I'd always be his little princess. When the fairy tale ended, though, I grew up. And then he didn't want me anymore."

Morgan thought for a moment. "Maybe it wasn't that he didn't want you, Katie. Maybe he assumed that you wouldn't want him. That he hurt you and your mother too much. Maybe he thinks he's not good enough for you."

Softly sliding her fingers along the tree house wall, Katie answered after considering the idea. "Hmmm, I don't know. Maybe." She sighed and threw her elbows back to lock her hands behind her head. In doing so, however, she knocked Morgan with her elbow.

"Whoa! That's my nose, you know," he exclaimed as he rubbed it. "It could use a little straightening, though. Maybe you helped it out."

Katie turned to get a closer look. "You're right, I think it does look better now," she teased. "Sorry, Morgan. Does it still hurt?"

"Nah, just a little," Morgan answered. "But if that's the price for lying next to you in a tree house, I'll pay it any time."

Katie chuckled and turned again to gaze through the missing board in the roof.

"I think," she joked, "that the only way we're ever going to find out about my dad is if we ask him straight out. We could go inside and call—my mom has his number now. Should we do it?" Katie laughed.

Morgan looked way too serious. "Not today. But someday, maybe. Someday I just might ask him."

As Katie and Morgan grew silent, the branches, leaves, and wind surrounding the tree house made soft, mixed noises: the spinning of leaves against each other, the scraping of branches along the walls, and a far away, hushed whir of wind among the topmost branches. Light leaked through the missing slat, causing shadows of leaves to dance over their clothes and skin.

"When I drove you home from church on Sunday, you said you might ask your mother if they named you after your ancestor Katherine. Did you ask her?" questioned Morgan, breaking the silence.

"I did ask her. She said that when I was born, my dad's grandfather noticed that I had the same birthmark his grandmother had—it looked kind of like a solar-eclipsed sun. Mine is sort of faded now." Katie turned away from Morgan and pulled her hair away from the back of her neck. "Do you see it?"

"Wow! It does look like a solar eclipse—just way in miniature. How many people are born with something like that printed on their neck?"

"Well," said Katie, turning back around, "this grandfather really wanted them to name me after her, and so they did. Katherine May McBride. Her maiden name was Devonshire."

Morgan blinked several times as light shone directly into his eyes. "So she was, well, she is your great, great-grandmother."

"Right. I prefer to think of her as 'is.' Because, well . . . , because she 'is.' She changed my life. She helped me find what was missing."

Morgan turned his face to Katie's and chuckled. "Wouldn't it be funny if she were listening to us right now?"

Katie smiled. "I hope she is."

"It's crazy, Katie. The whole thing is crazy."

"You know what, though?" Morgan added. "If it weren't for Katherine Devonshire McBride, I wouldn't be anywhere near you. Without her, Katie, you would have hitchhiked to New York by now."

They were quiet for a moment, and then Morgan spoke cautiously. "So, Katie," he began, "there is something I wanted to talk to you about. I'll be nineteen in January. I'll be going on a mission in just five or six months, you know."

Katie chuckled and rolled her eyes. "Oh, my gosh, Morgan. Of course I know. You've only mentioned it to me a hundred times this summer." She laughed.

"You're right. I probably have. I can't believe, though, that summer is almost over. You'll be back to school in just a couple of weeks!"

"And I have two years left to do it right. Do you think, Morgan, that colleges look at real improvement in grades? I mean, what if I get a 4.0 from here on out? Will they just average my ninth through twelfth grade GPA's and call it good?"

"If you get a 4.0 for the next two years, Katie, guaranteed they'll notice it."

Katie smiled and clasped her hands behind her head again—this time carefully.

"Katie—I'll be gone for two whole years. A lot could happen in two years."

"Aha! I understand." Katie laughed. "I get it! You want me to wait for you! Morgan, really. With all the guys lined up way down the street just to see me, how will I ever be able to wait for you?" she joked.

Morgan turned to his side and propped his head up with his elbow. "I mean, I don't care if you go on dates, Katie. I want you to! But if you find someone you want to marry, just promise me you'll wait until I get back. I've never met anyone like you before, and, well . . . I just feel like I'm the one who is supposed to be with you—always, I mean."

For a minute Katie lost her breath. Her heart jumped hard

or skipped a beat or something, and she had to take a deep breath to catch it back. "Are you serious?" she asked finally.

"Dead serious," responded Morgan.

Katie thought for a moment. "Well, do you promise to fix the broken board up there?" she finally asked.

"I promise. I kind of like the sunlight, though. Are you sure you want it fixed?"

"No," answered Katie. "I'm not sure. But if I want it fixed, will you fix it?"

"Yes, whenever you say, ma'am."

"Okay." Katie laughed. "You know I'm only sixteen, though, and getting married is the last thing on my mind—I don't even want to think about it until I'm done with college! But . . . well . . . if you promise, I promise."

Morgan smiled and looked straight into Katie's black, Irish eyes. "There's just something about you, Katie. From the moment I first saw you. I wish I had a video of you swinging your bucket high as you walked up to us. I thought then that what you really wanted to do was swing it right into the bushes!" he said with a chuckle. "And your smile—it twisted up on one side. I wondered what on earth you were thinking—what you knew that I didn't. And your hair, well . . . it just exploded with sun! Really!" he added as Katie laughed. "And I couldn't stop staring into your eyes. I still can't. I feel like I've known you forever."

Realizing she felt exactly the same way, Katie grew quiet. The tree house seemed far away from the world, almost on another planet. She closed her eyes and listened to the leaves and branches and wind. Katie had never felt such peace. It was almost as if her arms and legs might melt through the wooden floor.

"You're so beautiful, Katie," Morgan said as he slid a thick strand of her dark hair through his fingers. Then, after a moment of hesitation, he leaned closer to Katie's lips, and softly, very softly, he kissed her.

Scriptures and Sources

1. 2 Nephi 1:23
2. Doctrine and Covenants 136:1–2
3. "Nellie Unthank: Despite hardship, 'she gave more than she received,'" *Church News* (August 10, 1991), as quoted by David O. McKay from *Relief Society Magazine*, January 1948, p. 8.
4. Isaiah 7:2
5. Carol Cornwall Madsen, *Journey to Zion: Voices from the Mormon Trail* (Salt Lake City: Deseret Book, 1997), 658–660.
6. Coke Newell, *Latter Days: An Insider's Guide to Mormonism, The Church of Jesus Christ of Latter-day Saints* (New York: St. Martin's Griffin, 2001), 195.
7. Matthew 11:28
8. "Come, Come, Ye Saints," *Hymns*, 30.

About the Author

Debra Terry Hulet grew up in Las Vegas, Nevada. After her graduation from Brigham Young University with a BA in English literature and a minor in Spanish language, she lived in Venezuela for eight years. Upon returning to the United States, she taught secondary English and elementary and secondary Spanish.

Independence Rock is Mrs. Hulet's first published work. She resides in Utah with her family.